WAR ORIGIN

C.G. HARRIS

Join the C.G. Harris Legion

Join the C.G. Harris Legion to receive book intel, useless trivia, special giveaways, free books, plus you'll learn about Hula Harry and get his Drink of the Week.

https://www.cgharris.net/legion-sign-up-page

Working for The Judas Agency was like waking up every morning knowing you had to get a root canal—with no anesthesia. The job had to be done, but unless you're some kind of crazy, tooth sadist, you knew your day was really going to suck.

"What do you mean start a war?" I jogged to keep up with my partner, Alex. She wore her usual Topside attire: long boots, black trench coat, jeans, and a tee with strategic wear-holes to display the myriad of tattoos on her milky white skin. Her long hair, pulled back in a ponytail, read all business were it not for the Ty-D-Bol blue color. My style wasn't as edgy as Alex's. Brown and orange patchwork Gore-Tex and a buzzcut. Great for durability, but it wouldn't get me a red-carpet interview at the Emmys.

"I don't want to start a war in the middle of Los Angeles."

We had dropped into the city looking for an out of the way place to carry out our mission. When I say dropped in, I mean we used the Envisage Splice, a nausea inducing transport that allowed us to travel from The Nine—a cheery spin on Dante's euphemism for the deepest depths of Hell—to the land of sunshine and breathing. And right now, it was the breathing that was giving me trouble.

"Can we slow down?" I said between breaths. "I don't think qualifying for the L.A. Marathon is part of our mission."

"Sorry." Alex slowed from her power walking pace to that of a grocery store stroll. "I just want to beat the noonday lunch rush. Another hour and we would be waist deep in suits, construction workers, and bicycle couriers."

I took a moment to catch my breath. We were dead. It didn't seem fair that we should still get tired. Technically speaking, I shouldn't even have to breathe, but here I was, wheezing like the little train that could after a few blocks of smog wogging.

"You should get in better shape." Alex raised an eyebrow at me as I paced along beside her. "I'm not saying you need to be an Olympian, but this is ridiculous."

"I work out at least five-ish times a week." It was true. Ever since Alex had started training me in the fine arts of fist to face fighting, I had decided a little cardio wouldn't hurt. I had no idea why I sucked wind now.

"Well, next time you're on the treadmill, try turning it on. They work much better if you're not just standing on it."

I shot her a narrow-eyed glare. "Can we get back to the question at hand?" Alex rolled her eyes in obvious frustration. "We're not starting a real war. Sabnack sent us on a mission to stir up discontent among the local street gangs, that's all. It's not like we're carpet bombing Hollywood Boulevard, so relax."

Sabnack was our department supervisor. Half man, half lion, all demon. He assigned us to our delightful missions to create havoc and mayhem on behalf of The Judas Agency.

"I never thought I would be relieved to hear the words 'gang war.'" I nodded.

"I'm so glad you feel better. Now can we get moving? We aren't in the best part of town." She sped up but kept a more reasonable pace than she had before.

Now it was my turn to scoff as I caught up with her. "They can't hurt us. What are you worried about?"

As long as we were Topside, any injury would heal instantly. At least anything caused by normal means. There were a few things that could harm a Niner, a Woebegone visiting from The Nine, but I was betting a typical bystander wouldn't have our brand of kryptonite on hand.

"I am less worried about us and more worried about them. What if some idiot shoots you in the face for talking too much? Which is a real possibility by the way. Should we lay waste to the whole town? Plus, how would you explain the fact that you came out of it looking as ugly as always."

"Ouch." I rubbed my face with my hand. "You think I talk too much?"

Alex rolled her eyes again and kept walking.

"So how many people are we talking about? I mean with the whole gang thing. I know it's not a full-scale war but..."

I trailed off as we rounded the corner of a high-rise building and wandered right into the middle of a huge crowd of people. I couldn't believe I had missed all the chatter and chanting. Maybe I did talk too much.

Alex and I backpedaled a few steps and slid off to the side, watching as they walked by. Many of them carried signs that read things like *Our Body, Our Right* and *Lockdown Government Poison*. They all wore surgical masks, bandanas, or face coverings of one kind or another and passed out flyers to anyone who would accept them.

I looked over at Alex. "This is not going to help our low profile."

One of the surgical mask bandits offered me a bright orange flyer, so I took it and read the bold title.

The headline said, "Stop MiRACL."

Alex read the blocked letters over my shoulder as well. The name made us both glance up and lock eyes. Earlier in the year we had a major run-in with the corporation, along with its new CEO and President, Ryan Rokuda.

To be accurate, it wasn't Ryan at all, but rather a fellow resident of The Nine named Simeon Scott. He had possessed Ryan and hijacked not only his body but also his company and had exploited his revolutionary medical breakthroughs ever since. Alex and I had seen Ryan push past Simeon's spirit for a moment and plead for help on national T.V., proving he was still a prisoner inside his body. We had been looking for a way to help him ever since. Easier said than done considering we had no idea how to extract the spirit of a Niner from a living human, and I was under strict orders from my boss, the one and only Judas Iscariot, to stay far away from Simeon/Ryan altogether.

The whole thing was insane, and now MiRACL had developed what they believed was the cure for all disease in our generation. A self-replicating nanite that not only adapted to a human's health needs, but it also spread through the air like a common cold, inoculating new people with nanites each time a carrier came into contact with the general population.

On one hand, it seemed like a modern miracle, pun intended, spreading like a micro autonomous superhero to cure disease on its own. On the other hand, MiRACL invaded peoples' bodies without their permission, and Americans in particular were not happy about it. Once released, it would only be a matter of time before the nanites reached every man, woman, and child on the planet, whether they wanted them or not. If there was one thing Americans would not stand for, it was someone taking away their right to choose.

"I heard about this," Alex said. "I didn't know they planned to demonstrate today, but they've been holding protests all over the country. Apparently, the U.K. had a Smallpox outbreak. No one can explain it since the disease has been wiped out for years. People up here think Ryan ... Simeon had something to do with it. They believe he weaponized the Smallpox in order to back them into a corner. I hear he's moved his whole base of operations to Europe, and they are planning to release his self-propagating nanites to fight the disease."

The protest grew in intensity as Alex spoke. They chanted, screamed, and began to march over the top of cars and bang on windows. The crowd was beginning to turn ugly. Invulnerable or not, I wasn't sure I wanted to be here when this thing turned from protest to angry mob. These people just needed a primer to set off the explosion.

"Hey." A female voice rose out of the crowd. I searched the sea of people and landed on a woman who marched straight toward us. I felt Alex tense next to me.

The stranger was at least as tall as me, if not taller. Athletic and assertive. She wore baggy jeans that were a little short, a dark shirt, and peacoat so black it seemed to swallow the sunlight. Her stark white spiked hair matched her eyebrows and eyelashes, a glaring contrast to her dark, accusing eyes.

"You two." She raised an arm and pointed a finger in our direction. "You work for them. You work for MiRACL. I saw you on television with Ryan Rokuda." She looked around at the crowd then yelled, "They're spying on us. Get them!"

CHAPTER TWO

Alex and I both held our hands up as the incensed crowd seemed to turn on us in unison.

"Take it easy now." I couldn't help but take a step back. "We don't even know this person."

I looked around for our persecutor, but she had vanished into the growing mob. "We're just here to join your demonstration. Down with MiRACL." I held up a fist in protest, but my gesture was met by narrowed eyes.

"Where are your masks?" A lanky looking man in front of the crowd poked a finger toward our faces. "If you're with us, why aren't you wearing a mask?"

I shrugged, searching for a plausible answer. "My dog ate it?"

Lanky shook his head. "You're sympathizers. You're probably even carriers."

The crowd seemed to pause at that, and Alex seized on the subtle cue.

"That's right. We work for MiRACL, and we were sent here to propagate the nanites to any protesters we ran into. We're here to help you see the truth, induct you into the future of medicine, so even our most stubborn opponents will become advocates."

In a move so swift I hardly saw it, Alex slid forward and swept her hand up to tug at Lanky's mask. It fell away, and Alex blew a puff of air in his face.

"Thanks for being first in line."

Lanky lurched away so hard he almost toppled over backward, and he wasn't the only one. The entire crowd fell back on its heels as Alex took in a deep breath as if she were a dragon ready to spew fire. Everyone paused for a moment in time, waiting to see what the other would do, then Alex blew out her air, and the crowd went running.

Alex began to cackle before she ran out of breath. I pulled her back into an alley, away from the main street where the protesters were already regrouping to continue their march, this time with a wary eye for any more MiRACL interlopers. Sooner or later, they would realize they had just run away from a wheezing, blue-haired woman for no reason, and I didn't want to be standing there when they did.

"I can't believe you got away with that." A laugh of my own escaped my lips. "They ran like you were going to vomit an army of mini-Terminators."

"We would have needed an army to fight our way out of that mess. Come on, we need to get back on task." Alex turned and started off at a slow jog.

I followed, not wanting to be left behind.

"What was with that Q-tip, trouble-maker anyway? She rats us out for no reason then disappears?"

"Maybe she was just a concerned citizen," I panted.

Alex turned a corner at the end of the block and jogged up the street.

I loped in behind her, already wearing down. This breathing thing was really getting old.

I opened my mouth to reason that the crowd was far

enough away that we didn't have to run anymore, when Q-tip leapt out of a building in front of us, arms extended, and teeth bared in a snarl.

Alex reacted first. Instead of skidding to a stop, she side-stepped our attacker and dove past her, rolling to her feet at the woman's back.

I made a much less graceful stop, squeaking my shoes on the sidewalk like a basketball player caught in a three-way screen.

In the end, we had our attacker surrounded front and back before she could take her first swing.

"Whoa, whoa," she said. "Take it easy. I was just fooling around."

I had my fists up ready to fight, and I thought Alex might take the cheap shot at the back of her head out of spite.

"That crowd wasn't fooling around," Alex growled. "If you're trying to be funny, your standup needs a lot of work."

Our new interloper held her hands into the air and smiled. "Fair enough. Perhaps my little prank wasn't all that funny. I just figured a crowd of mortals wouldn't be much of a problem for the likes of you two." The corners of her lips grew into a wry smile, and she turned so she could see the both of us. "Don't worry. Your little secret is safe with me."

Neither of us put our hands down, but Alex's posture became less punchy and more suspicious. "Who are you?"

The stranger dropped her arms and opened her coat to bow with a flourish. "I am Samyaza, although my friends call me Sammy."

I eyed her, trying to work out if her name should mean something to me. When she received nothing but silence at her introduction, she let out a sigh and slumped a little from her royal stature.

"I am what you would call an angel. I have been relegated to this rotted dominion for longer than dirt has had a name, and when I happen upon those with a fellow—shall we say, creative impermanence—I like to say hello."

My hands fell to my sides, and I looked Sammy up and down.

"You're an angel?" I panted out, still out of breath from my run.

She crossed her arms over her chest. "So sorry to disappoint. My wings and halo are at the cleaners, but maybe this will help."

Samyaza flung her arm out, and in her hand, she manifested a sword made of pure, molten fire. I carried a Denarius coin that did something similar once, manifesting a battle-axe made of flame for me to fight off an enemy, but this was something different. This was pure light and power. White hot as the sun and twice as formidable. One swing of that sword could bring down armies, and somehow, this human-shaped being held it in her hand as if the incredible weapon were no more than a wisp of wind.

With a snap of her wrist, the sword disappeared as fast as it had come, and the street felt empty without it. I had never witnessed anything so extraordinary or forbidding, and frankly, I hoped to never see anything like it again.

"Well, now that that's over, what are you crazy kids up to?"

CHAPTER THREE

Samyaza ... Sammy, beamed at the two of us like a kindergarten teacher on the first day of class. Alex and I, in turn, stared back at her with uncertainty and suspicion. It wasn't every day that you met an angel, especially where we lived, but she looked more like a homeless dock worker than an agent of the heavens. Granted, she had a bit of style, and her shocking white hair stood out in a crowd. But nothing about the woman before us cried out angelic.

"No offense, but is there something we can do for you?" Alex relaxed a bit from her attack posture, but she still looked ready to leap like a cat if anyone so much as sneezed.

Sammy rolled her head around in exasperation. "I shouldn't have shown you the gladius. I knew it. I pull out the gladius, and everyone gets all twitchy. I just wanted to hang out, say hello. I'm tired of wandering around with all these flash paper mortals down here. They think their lives are so important. They live eighty years, if they're lucky, then poof. You and I know where the real time is spent. This is just incubation, and they're a bunch of eggs waiting to hatch."

I realized my eyes had grown wide enough to shove my

eyebrows out of the way, so I blinked a few times to return them to a normal size.

"Aren't you supposed to be good and compassionate and all that?" I said. "I mean, far be it from me to tell you how to do your job, but it feels like you're a little off base here."

Sammy snorted out a laugh. "Pick up a Bible some time. We don't come down to sprinkle flower petals and recite poetry to orphans. We smite, we battle, we punish. If heaven had bouncers, they would be angels."

A laugh escaped my lips before I could catch it at the image of a tattoo clad angel standing at the pearly gates in a black t-shirt and sunglasses.

"That still doesn't answer why you're here." Alex wore a hint of a grin on her face as well.

"Pure chance." Sammy ushered us both forward in the direction we had been walking before she had stopped us and fell in step behind. "I'm glad I ran into you though. Sorry about my little prank with the crowd. After a few millennia, I guess my sense of humor can be a little off."

Alex gave her a slow nod as she strolled forward. "We try to stay under the radar. Mixing it up with dozens of protesters would be a little hard to explain to the higher-ups."

"So, you're on the job up here? What do you do? Who are you working for?"

Alex and I stared at each other, realizing Sammy might know where we were from but not our creative career choice. Telling the smiting hand of Heaven that we were there on behalf of The Judas Agency to wreak havoc on humanity could stretch the limits of our Topside invincibility health plan.

Sammy stared at us for a moment then let out a laugh. "Take it easy. I know you're Judas Agents." Sammy reached up and fingered the pin on Alex's lapel. It was the key to accessing the Envisage Splice and coming Topside. Only Judas Agents would possess such a thing. "Sorry. Like I said, my sense of humor is—" She made a twirly motion with her finger next to her ear.

"What's your mission? Are you spreading a plague, plotting an assassination? You can tell me. I have been off the clock for—"

She looked at her wrist which bore no watch.

"About three thousand years. I promise I won't tell."

My jaw fell open. "Three thousand years?"

"Give or take. We have a loose interpretation on career postponement."

I shook my head. "That's a long time to mingle with mankind, I have to admit. I've only been dead forty years, and it feels like forever."

Sammy scoffed. "Infants. Come talk to me when you pass your first thousand."

We kept walking, but Alex had slowed our speed to a near crawl. I was thankful for the slackened pace because I was still having a little trouble catching my breath from our run. Maybe there should be a moving treadmill in my future.

I guessed we were near our destination, but Alex wasn't all that keen on having an angel tag along. She dragged her feet, no doubt hoping the wayward angel would leave, or we would come up with a reason for her to go. Sammy just smiled at us as if she were oblivious to the entire situation.

"Look," Alex finally said. "It was great to meet you and all, but we need to do our job and ..."

"Oh, come on." Sammy interrupted. "Please don't kick me out. I never get to have any fun. I can even help. I'm very sneaky. Do we need to kidnap a dignitary's child or slit someone's throat? Whatever it is, I'm in."

I gaped at Alex and then back at Sammy.

"What?" Sammy raised an eyebrow. "When you've lived as long as I have, everything seems a little vanilla."

"Slitting someone's throat is vanilla?" I wiped the sweat off my head and dried my hand on my pants. "I would hate to hear what you think is extreme."

Alex stopped for a second and looked at me as if she expected some way out of our predicament.

"What are we going to do?" I shrugged. "It's not like we can kick an angel out of the party. You might as well tell her what we're up to."

Alex sighed and turned a corner to walk toward a large brick building. Instead of heading for the front, we ducked into the alley off to the side, so we wouldn't be as noticeable to any passersby.

"Fine. Our job is to incite fighting among local street gangs. The Agency wants to keep them at odds with one another, so crime rates stay on the rise within the city."

Sammy rubbed her hands together. "Nice. The Judas Agency always was a big picture sort of organization. So, what's your part in this whole thing? Are you going to dress up as gang members and do a drive by? No, I'll bet you're here to take out one of the leaders. That's why you're not in gang garb. You want to fly in under the radar and take them out, maybe plant some evidence, then zap back to the creature comforts of the under-world. This is going to be so fun."

Sammy clapped her hands in excited little jerks while Alex stopped to stare at her. If the creative violence evoked by her imagination got any more vanilla, we would be staging a mass murder by sundown.

"No, none of that is going to happen. We are working on something more subtle."

Alex opened her coat and pulled out a couple of spray paint cans and a file folder from an inside pocket. She tossed one of the cans to me and opened the folder to reveal a series of graffiti photos.

"We're going to use these."

CHAPTER FOUR

Sammy scooted around to get a look at the file contents, and as soon as she laid eyes on the pictures, she let out a gale of laughter.

"Graffiti? That's your big plan?" More laughing as Alex and I stood there holding our spray cans.

"Wow." Sammy wiped a tear out of her eye and took a deep breath. "The Disaster Factory has definitely lost a bit of its edge if spray-paint is the big gun in their arsenal."

Alex sneered, showing her teeth. "The Judas Agency is smart enough to know how to remain invisible while inflicting the maximum amount of damage. There's a reason no one on Earth has ever heard of us. We are the deadliest terrorist organization ever devised, and we do it without ever getting caught. So yes, spray paint can be one of The Agency's big guns. So long as it achieves the desired effect, it might as well be a nuclear bazooka."

Sammy held up her hands in placation. "No offense meant. I am just used to bloodied swords and mayhem. Finger paint seems a little beneath you."

Alex gritted her teeth and sort of half smiled, half growled.

"It's spray paint, not finger paint, and we don't need to compensate with a big flaming sword to convince violent gang members to start infighting."

Alex stared Sammy down, but Sammy didn't seem to notice. She continued to smile with that innocent look of enthusiasm, even if it wasn't quite as eager as before.

I figured I had better change the subject before Alex decided to test how angelic Sammy really was.

"I don't know why we're up here trying to make gangs fight each other anyway. Unless things have changed since I left in the eighties, they do a pretty good job of killing each other on their own."

Sammy walked over and perched herself against a bike rack at the edge of the street while Alex did her best to ignore the fact that she was there at all. She turned her back on Sammy and consulted her photos then began painting with swift sweeps of her arm.

"Actually, things have changed since you rode the escalator down to the underground floor." Sammy watched Alex as she spoke, and I prayed she wouldn't offer any artistic critiques.

"Gangs used to be all about who controlled what areas, but now it's more about controlling a market. They still dominate their territories, but one gang might have the corner on guns, while the other has drugs or human trafficking. They control markets on everything you can think of—crooked business deals, money laundering, protection. You name it, one gang or another controls it."

Sammy lifted a finger to point out something on the wall where Alex painted, but I stepped in front of her to block her view.

"So how does that keep them from fighting?"

"Easy," she said, giving up on whatever critique she was about to offer. "They all have something the other one wants. One gang has guns but wants drugs. So they trade, and everyone is happy. As long as there is a supply and demand, they all work together. And no one wants outside gangs moving into their city, so it keeps them from reaching out of their area for trade as well. It's a gangland economic paradise."

I shook my head in disbelief and turned to head over to the wall with my own spray can. "I can't believe things have changed that much."

"Imagine what it will be in another forty years," Alex said. "Now, are you going to help me or stand there talking all day?"

I shook my can, and the metal bearing inside rattled the paint ready for me to spray.

"What do I do?"

Alex handed me an 8x10 photo of some gang graffiti.

"Paint this, and don't screw it up. We don't have erasers for this stuff."

Alex went to turn away and then noticed my hands. Saying they were chapped and cracked was an understatement. Over the past couple of weeks, the skin on my knuckles had begun to crack, and ugly, dark scabs had formed in their place. Sores had even appeared on the back of my hand. I had managed to hide the manicurist's nightmare, thinking I would get around to finding a way to clear it up on my own, but now Alex had seen them. There would be no ignoring it any longer.

"What is the deal with that?" She pointed at my hand and shot me a disgusted look.

I pulled away and hid my cracked, ugly skin from sight. "Just dry, that's all. A little lotion, and I'll be as good as new."

Alex eyed me. "How many Woebegone have you seen with hands like that? Let me see them again."

I hesitated.

"Come on. Let me see." She motioned for me to bring my hands out of hiding.

I let out a breath and held them out for inspection.

Sammy came up beside me to peer down at them too. "Esh.

That's going to take more than a little lotion, my friend. You need a grand master of dermatology to help you with that."

Alex gave her a look but didn't respond. "How do you feel? Has anything weird been happening?"

I slumped back against the wall, realizing I still hadn't recovered from our short jog. Something might be very wrong, but I wasn't ready to admit it to Alex, especially in front of our new angelic guest.

"I just get a little tired," I said, downplaying the obvious. "Sometimes I can't catch my breath."

Truth was, I felt like I had run across half the continent. My legs were all burning Jell-O, and the buildings around us were beginning to spin. The longer I resisted the urge to rest, the harder it got to remain standing.

"How much have you used your Topside powers?"

Every Agent in The Nine manifested a power when they returned Topside. It was a well-kept secret and usually had something to do with their past life. For me, I could rust things. Not all that flashy, but I had used it to rust through the main supports of a railroad bridge a few weeks ago to keep a train from derailing into a town. It had been a stretch for my powers to say the least. If this turned out to be some sort of blowback, it was something I had never heard about before.

"The girders on that bridge were pretty thick. I had to rust through a lot of them to bring the thing down."

My voice began to sound sleepy and a little slurred. I shook my head and blinked several times to try and wake myself up, but the sidewalk seemed to spin under my feet.

"We need to get you back down to The Agency. Sammy can you help me—"

Alex looked around. When she didn't finish her sentence, I peered up as well, which made the world almost spin out of control.

"Yo! What are you two doing?"

Despite my tilt-a-whirl optics, I surmised two things: one, Sammy was nowhere to be found, and two, we were about to be joined by four young strangers walking up behind us.

All of the young men were Latino and wore cuffed pants and white t-shirts. One had a gold baseball cap turned to the side, and all of them had the sort of ink you'd find in a prison yard rather than a tattoo shop.

As soon as they crossed the street, I crumbled to my knees on the sidewalk, leaving Alex to stare down the four gang members all alone.

CHAPTER FIVE

"Do you know where you are?" Gold Cap took a step forward and circled us, eyeing the graffiti and our paint cans. I made an attempt to get off the ground but didn't have the strength and wound up back on my butt, staring up at their smirking faces again.

"You're either the dumbest tourists I've ever seen, or our rivals are lowering their standards for recruitment."

They all laughed and pounded each other's fists.

"Your friend huff too much of that paint down there? He have a wallet full of cash and credit cards? I'm sure we can help him find his way home."

They all laughed again.

Alex crouched down next to me, ignoring the circling gang of jackals.

"Can you stand up?" She spoke at a near whisper next to my ear.

I shook my head. "How about a pyro show?"

Alex could manifest fire the way I could rust metal. When superpowers had been handed out in Hell, she had gotten into the cool line.

Alex shook her head to that idea too. "Normally I wouldn't worry about getting hurt, but you're in no shape to pick a fight."

"Enough whispers." Gold Cap circled around in front of us and moved in so close his toes touched my knees. "Get up."

Alex stood. I tried to stand up again but only managed to rise about six inches before collapsing to the concrete again.

"Your boyfriend there really knows how to party. How 'bout you?" Gold Cap stepped in closer to Alex and grinned. "You like to party?"

Alex didn't give up a millimeter of ground. She just stood there, staring Gold Cap down as his friends rounded in to stand behind him.

Why did I have to go limp right now? Alex needed me, and all I could do was stare up at them like a lost puppy. One swift boot, and I would be flat on my back counting my teeth.

"Listen," Alex said, her voice never wavering. "We're here to do a job. It's nothing personal."

Gold Cap and his boys laughed. "You hear that boys? It's nothing personal."

He turned his stare back to Alex again. "Tell me, why is your job nothing personal to us when you're in our territory?"

"I mean, some guy hired us to come down here and paint this stuff all over the walls. Look."

Alex turned to pick up the file folder full of glossy photographs. "See, they even gave us pictures to go by."

Gold Cap took the folder and passed it back to one of his minions, never taking his eyes off of Alex.

"She's right," the guy with the folder said. "These are all gang signs."

"So, who was this mysterious stranger who hired you?" Gold Cap looked Alex up and down. "Our rivals are capable of tagging anything they want, and they don't need a bunch of pictures to do it. They wouldn't hire a couple of amateurs like you. There's no pride in it."

Alex kept her expression stone cold.

"I didn't say another gang hired us. It was some suit. He said we didn't look the part, so we wouldn't get caught as long as we were careful. I guess he was wrong."

"A suit."

Gold Cap said it more as a statement than a question. I thought the story sounded pretty thin, but for whatever reason, it struck a chord with this guy.

"Where did he hire you? How did he get a hold of you?"

"I don't know, man." Alex did a good job of sounding like a perp being questioned by the cops. "It was downtown somewhere. My boyfriend and I were hanging out, and he got out of his car and offered us a hundred bucks to do the job. We hit the liquor store then came here."

She added the tiniest hint of a slur to her voice. Just enough that they might wonder if it had been there the whole time.

"What kind of car?"

Alex shrugged. "Dark sedan. He got out of the back seat, that's all I know. Look, you can have all this stuff. We didn't mean any harm. It was just a job."

Gold Cap pointed to the spray cans on the sidewalk next to the wall. "Cover up those signs. Legit or not, they can't be in our territory. And you two." Gold Cap turned his attention back to us again.

"This is our territory. If we ever see you here again, we'll kill you. Now beat it."

"You're going to let them go?" one of Gold Cap's minions whined.

He glared back at him. "We have business to take care of. Now, do what I told you, and don't question me."

Minion went to work without another word, picking up one of our cans to cover up our crude artwork with his own.

Alex didn't wait for a second invitation to leave. She crouched down and threw my arm over her shoulder. With a heave and a stagger, we managed to stand together amongst the giggles and snickers of the hardened gang members. I didn't care. Alex had talked our way into freedom, and I was happy to have it at any price. I just had to hope this leg jelly wasn't a permanent condition.

CHAPTER SIX

I slumped on the bench in The Judas Agency locker room, elbows on my knees, staring down at the gray tiled floor. I had already changed out of my Topside gear and back into my usual t-shirt and pair of 501 button-fly Levi's. Alex stowed her gear into her tall, black lockers as well. She didn't have much to change. She just shed her jacket and boots and kept the peek-a-boo t-shirt and jeans.

She plopped down next to me on the bench and shoved her feet into a more fashionable pair of high heeled boots that matched the color of her hair.

"I'm glad to see you're able to at least sit up on your own now. Why didn't you tell me something was wrong?"

I looked over at her. "I didn't really know till I hit the sidewalk out there. I've felt a little tired, but even today, I figured I was just worn out from our run from the crowd. I'm not all that worried about it though. It'll pass. A full night's rest, and I'll be as good as new."

Alex stopped mid-pull on her second boot. "You collapse in the middle of a gang filled street like a jellyfish out of water for no discernible reason, and you're not all that worried? If you

23

were alive, you'd be sitting in an emergency room giving them half your blood while they hooked you up to a thousand wires and body scanned you from head to toe."

"I'd like to see them do that now." I chuckled. "I wonder what they'd find?"

"They would find a moron." Alex finished pulling on her boot and stomped her foot down. "I've heard of something like this before."

She reached out to grab my wrist and forced me to stare at the dry, cracked skin on the back of my hand. It looked red and irritated. It was painful, which was disturbing enough. We were dead. We had to worry about a lot of things but getting sick was not typically one of them.

"Overuse of your Topside power can damage you somehow." She tossed my hand back down on my lap. "Not just on the outside. That's only a byproduct. It can break you apart in some way I don't understand. It's rare, and not many have ever seen it."

"So how do we fix it? Is there an ointment or human-glue I can use to hold things together until I can fight this off?"

Alex stood up and slammed her locker so hard the sound made me jump.

"You don't get it. There's no cure for this. At least not one that I know of. It either goes away, or it doesn't."

"And what if it doesn't?"

Alex didn't look at me. "I don't know. I'm going to go back to my office and do some research. You should get some rest."

"While you're skating on your inter-web-thingy, why don't you poke around and see if there's a way we can tear Simeon out of Ryan's body? Preferably with lots of pain and suffering ... for Simeon, not Ryan, of course."

She walked over to the community clothing bins and rummaged through the crates on the floor. It was a sort of Agency closet for anyone to use. They had lots of different clothes for Agents who needed a little something extra to go Topside. Most of it seemed to be straight out of a hobo's wardrobe, but every once in a while, you could score a gem or two.

"First, it's called surfing the web." She enunciated the adage as if she were trying to explain The Three Little Pigs to a puppy. "Second, don't you think I have already done that? The Agency database has information on a lot of things but ways to escape the underworld is not one of them. If we are going to figure out how to yank Simeon out of his comfy Topside possession, we are on our own here."

Alex shook something out in her hand and then tossed them to me from the community stockpile. "Put those on. You don't want anyone else noticing your hands until we can figure out what to do about your—condition. As I want to help Ryan, you need to be worried about yourself right now. Let's figure out how to fix you, then we will get back to solving Ryan's problem."

I snatched the pair of gloves out of the air and looked them over. They were black, fingerless jobs with mesh backing, and they were pretty much brand new. I was no fashion fanatic, but even I knew gloves like this went out with Michael Jackson and big hair bands. On the other hand, I had died in the eighties and wore 501 Jeans and a faded Scorpions t-shirt, so they were right up my alley.

"Sweet. See if you can dig out some black eyeliner, and it'll be like the old days."

Alex glared.

"Take it easy, I'm kidding. I'll wear the Twisted Sister mitts and lay low, I promise. But I am not going to forget about Ryan."

Alex seemed to lose a little of her steam and walked over to give me a hand getting up. I acted like I didn't need her help, but in truth, I was still pretty weak in the knees.

"Me either, but you need to listen to me." She held me by my shoulder and looked me in the eyes. The concern I saw there crushed any sarcastic defense I might have mounted against her. "The Agency is not in the business of employing Agents who are—" She trailed off without finishing the sentence. "Just keep this to yourself until I can figure out a way to help you, okay?"

I nodded. Alex pulled me in close and wrapped her arms around me in a hug. The warmth of her body washed the world away, and I slipped my arms around her. She pulled away almost before I could hug her back, and the feeling was gone, leaving me somehow emptier than I had been moments before.

Her eyes were full of so much worry it was hard for me to look at. "Go get some rest," she said in a soft voice. "I'll see you later."

With that, she headed out the door. I stood all alone wondering how serious this *condition* could be. Was it really all that bad to play with your Topside power? Was there such a thing as playing with it too much? Would I grow hair on my palms and go blind? It didn't make sense.

I decided Alex could do the research while I did the resting. Every bit of my energy had been sapped out of my body, and I was ready to sleep for a week to gain it back. I turned to head for my apartment, but a familiar buzz vibrated in my pocket. It was my Denarius coin.

When I had been recruited into The Judas Agency, it had not been under the most normal of circumstances. Judas Iscariot had summoned me personally. Much to my surprise, he did not want me as a typical Agent. He recruited me as a double agent, one of thirty secret operatives within The Agency who worked to prevent the very worst atrocities from ever happening.

As you can imagine, I had been a little taken aback. The leader of the Disaster Factory recruiting me to throw a wrench into his operations, but that's what happened. Now I worked under the radar. Even Alex didn't know my true agenda, and if I told her, the coin would suck my spirit into a netherworld void where I would spend the rest of eternity. It made things difficult in an Agency full of terrorists, but at least I got to do good things instead of bad. The downside—I worked directly for Judas Iscariot, and he had an affinity for knowing the very worst times to summon me to his office.

I fingered the Denarius in my pocket. It buzzed again with the page from Judas.

I sighed. Tired and sick, it didn't matter. When Judas called, I had learned never to keep him waiting.

CHAPTER SEVEN

The elevator opened onto the top floor of the tallest building in The Judas Agency complex. Judas Iscariot's personal penthouse office. The waiting area, all dark wood and dark leather, oozed evil ambiance. The sculptures, tapestries, and paintings depicting unending tortures and atrocities pulled together the whole "don't forget you're in hell" motif. At the end of it all was a reception desk, the likes of which you might see in a doctor's office—if the doctor were Hannibal Lector.

I approached the receptionist, doing my best not to look at the gruesome décor.

"How are you today, Patty?" The Woebegone woman sitting behind the desk peered up at me over her horn-rimmed glasses. She did not return my mirthful smile. Patty was a bill-board photo right out of the fifties. Beehive hairdo, bright red lipstick, and even wore her yellow sweater fastened at the top with a pearl button.

I also had no idea if her name was Patty. After all the times I had been in this office, she still refused to tell me her real name, so I had made a game out of trying to guess it every time I dropped by.

"Mr. Iscariot is expecting you."

I tilted my head at her, never losing my grin. "I'm sure he won't mind waiting a moment. Just don't tell him I'm here quite yet."

That drew more of a reaction than anything I had said thus far. Her eyes widened in a moment of shock, then she shook her head and regained her stony composure.

"It's your funeral."

"We never get a chance to chat, you and I," I said. "How have you been? Anything new happening with you? Do you enjoy your job here as Judas's personal assistant?"

She stared at me for a moment without reacting, and for a second, I thought she might not answer. But then she sighed and set down the paper she held in her hand.

"Fine ... no ... and yes, because I get to see you panic when I mention that I informed Judas of your arrival as soon as you stepped off the elevator."

I let out a little chuckle then caught the expression she still wore on her face—stone cold as an iceberg.

I tried not to trip over my own feet as I moved toward Judas's office door, doing my best not to run.

"That was a dirty trick, Betty." I pointed at her as I got to the door. She turned her attention back down to the papers on her desk, and I caught the hint of a smile on her face. I knew she had a sense of humor under that frosty exterior, even if it was at the expense of setting me up.

The door before me was another wonder of horrors and violence. Carvings depicted one horrifying historical event after another in startlingly lifelike timelines that ran from one side of the door to the other. I hated to look at it much less touch it, even to knock.

Thankfully, and also with no small amount of creep factor, the door opened all on its own before I could lay a single knuckle on the wood.

"Mr. Gantry. What is taking you so long?" the voice boomed from inside.

I tried to hurry into the room, but my feet and legs protested. Entering the office of Judas Iscariot was no small thing. The resulting action was a sort of staggered walk, as if I were going to jog in but had to drag a hundred pounds of fear in behind me at the last minute.

"I'm sorry, sir. I stopped to speak to your assistant outside for a moment."

Judas knitted his eyebrows together in what looked like a cross of anger and confusion.

"Did she page you to her office?"

I stood there with my mouth open for a second, then said, "No, sir. I was just saying hello."

Judas nodded and walked around to the front of his gigantic ebony desk. "A word of advice, she is not much for chatting, and I am not much on waiting for you to learn she does not like to chat. In the future, refrain from accosting my assistant with your irritation."

I nodded. "Got it. No irritating, waiting, chatting, or accosting."

He stared at me as if I were a greasy hair stuck to his T-bone steak. I added a little salute, hoping to jar him out of his trance. It worked ... sort of.

"Why are you wearing those gloves? They look ridiculous."

I peered down at my hands, which were mercifully covered by the black mesh and leather.

"You never know when you might have to move some boxes or drive a sweet looking sports car. I like to be prepared."

Judas glared at me for a moment then leaned back and shook his head, breathing in and out in a deliberate motion. Normally, he would have yelled himself purple by now. I was growing him.

Behind him stood his two most faithful companions and

creepiest of Hell spawn. Procel, an eight-foot pillar of dusky robes, horns, and glowing red eyes and Mastema, a crouching nightmare of claws, teeth, leather, and sensuous skin. She wore a dingy grey blindfold, seemingly to quell her insatiable urge to hunt, but somehow, she still tracked my every move. Both of them stood behind Judas every time I had been in his office, like a pair of Abrams tanks with their barrels pointed at my face. Ever present and always ready to do his bidding. I had been the target of that bidding more than once. It never gave me a cozy feeling to see them, here or anywhere.

"Tell me what you're working on for The Agency. Have you been given an assignment?" He motioned to a chair made of human bones positioned in front of his desk. I hated sitting in it, but there were no other options. And defying Judas one more time might hit that purple button after all, so I stifled a cringe and sat.

"Yes. We've been assigned to stir up some civil unrest among street gangs. We just got back from L.A., and things didn't quite go as planned. But in the end, I think we got our point across."

The chair wasn't the only horror in the room. Like the reception area, Judas's office was filled with an artistic collection of torture and fear. Sort of like Ripley's Believe It or Not, only with knives and rusty barbed wire. Everywhere my eyes went, there was another depiction of suffering and torment. I did my best to keep my eyes forward, focusing on his enormous desk instead.

Judas stared back at me without saying a word. After a long moment of silence, I began to wonder if someone had written a dirty limerick on my forehead.

"I am almost afraid to ask, but when you say it didn't go as planned ..."

He left the question open for me to finish. I took a breath

and mentally whitewashed the story as best I could to keep Judas from getting upset.

"We went up to tag a bunch of graffiti in rival gang territory, but we got caught."

I could see the vein in the middle of Judas's forehead begin to pulse. So I talked faster.

"We told them we were hired by someone to do the job, and I think they bought it. They let us go and headed off to report back to whoever it is gangs report back to."

I decided to omit the part about Sammy and my rather untimely nap in the middle of said activities. The bare bones were enough.

Judas nodded. "That was fast thinking on your part. Good work."

"I can't take credit for it. Alex was the one who thought on her feet. She came up with the cover story."

"All the same, you turned a bad situation around. After your last assignment, you need a win on this one."

I refrained from correcting him on the fact that our last assignment was not an assignment at all. We were free of all official responsibilities and were expected, by Agency policy, to freelance. Alex had come up with the idea to derail a train into a town full of people.

Judas had thought this was a great idea. While my position as a double agent required me to stop worldwide atrocities from happening, it also meant I had to maintain a believable cover story by allowing *some* bad things to happen. That's where my job got a little tougher than I liked to admit.

I couldn't allow the people in that town to die. Instead of going through with the plan, I had abused my Topside power to send the train into a ravine. Big win for me and the people of Bozeman, Montana, not so much for my Judas Agent cover story.

"That *accident*," he enunciated the word accident for

emphasis, "had better be a one-off event. You need to solidify your position here at The Agency, and this sounds like an excellent mission on which to do it. Casualties will not only be localized, they will most likely be limited to the demographic who perpetrates this sort of crime in the first place. You are only adding fuel to a burning fire."

I shrugged. "I suppose so."

Judas leaned back on his desk and eyed me. "See this through, Gabriel. No more good deeds. No more hero work."

"What if things grow out of hand or lots of people could get hurt? We should have a safe word. How about Albatross?"

Judas stared at me for a moment, unamused. "If there is a line to be crossed, I am sure you will find it. A Denarii Division Agent should accomplish his mission in a subtle fashion, something you still need to master. Just worry about completing your assignment without screwing it up."

"I can be subtle." I mumbled almost under my breath. "I can be the King of Subtle. I can be so subtle that—"

"Enough." Judas put his hand up and then clenched it into a fist before lowering it. "Get this job done and do it as if you were a regular Agent. I don't need you casting any more suspicion on The Agency after your last run in with The Council."

The Council of Seven was the highest authority in The Nine, except for the big S himself. Alex and I had inadvertently drawn their attention by snooping around Simeon Scott, the new CEO of MiRACL, and now the target of every activist in the United States.

The alliance between Simeon and The Council was disturbing enough, but our meddling had turned the eyes of The Council on Judas and his Agency ... or should have. Judas had expected a formal inquiry ever since that day, but it had never come. Sometimes waiting for the shoe to drop was worse than the boot hitting you right in the face.

"I won't let you down. No hero work on this assignment. I

will play it straight evil and destruction unless you tell me different."

Judas eyed me a little harder and crossed his arms over his chest. "I don't want you playing hero on any job unless I tell you different. You keep it rough and dirty, and that includes your off time as well. Do we understand each other?"

I couldn't help but glance back at Procel and Mastema. Not long ago, I had come looking for their help behind Judas's back to save a friend from a nasty demon and his clown-faced minions. I wondered how much they had told Judas, or if they had told him anything at all. I wouldn't give myself up that easy. Instead of asking questions, I just nodded.

"I understand. Nothing to bring any heat."

Judas flashed me his teeth in a smile, an expression almost as terrifying as his fury, then he rounded his desk to sit back in his plush high back leather chair again.

"If you have anything unusual to report, you know where to find me."

I took my cue and got up to leave as Judas reached for his raven's quill and began writing something on a piece of parchment.

I glanced back just before I walked out the door, and it was not Judas who caught my attention but Mastema. The normally docile, albeit creepy, demon motioned to me behind Judas's back. She pointed to me, then to her, then outside. I wasn't sure what she meant. Was I supposed to wait for her in the lobby? Not likely. What would she do, excuse herself to the little demon's room? I nod-shrugged a noncommittal response then disappeared out the door. If she wanted a taste of Gabe, she would have to come get it herself.

CHAPTER EIGHT

Going back to my Agency apartment to get some rest was the smart thing to do. It was the logical thing to do. After passing out Topside in the middle of an op that could have gotten Alex and I torn to shreds ... well, me at least ... it's what any reasonable person would do. It just wasn't what I was going to do.

I made my way outside and down the main stairs. The Judas Agency complex was made up of not one, but six buildings all arranged in a circular pattern. The first was six stories tall and each consecutive tower was six stories taller than the last, leaving a cobblestone courtyard in the center full of horrifying statues and murderous Agents, a wonderful, relaxing place to take a lunch break or afternoon tea. It was all quite impressive, which was the point. In a ruined landscape of suffering and destruction, The Judas Agency reigned supreme.

I was headed for the rear of the third tower. It had a hidden alcove where few, if any, Agents much less wondering Woebegone, would ever seek to explore. A perfect place in which to hide my little gem.

The oversized tricycle squeaked backward out of its

makeshift bike port, and I threw my leg over the seat and started pedaling. A good friend had given it to me as a gift. A way to traverse the dangers of The Nine without having to make my way on foot. She said it was designed to carry tools or equipment in areas like airports or third world countries. I just cared that it was strong, steady, and had a basket in the back big enough to haul half a body ... if one were inclined to make two trips.

I wound my way through the passages and streets of The Nine. They were littered with sheet metal and rusted steel that made up the building blocks of our shantied little existence. Woebegone built meager homes or businesses, then some disaster or demons would come through and tear it all down only so we could start again. It was the way of the afterlife for the damned. Build hope and steal it away. In some ways, it was the worst kind of torture. Too bad it wasn't the only one.

My trike always made the trip to Hula Harry's easier. It was a little slice of normalcy in the horrifying nightmare we called home. A bar built entirely of crushed cars. The place was not only durable, it happened to be one of the few places Woebegone could go to enjoy a bit of leisure that didn't entail disembowelment or torture. It was a sort of win-win for everyone.

I squeaked around a corner and made my way up another street, noticing that my energy reserves were dwindling faster than a social security check in a casino. My legs burned, and my lungs felt like they were trying to suck in poison gas made of razor blades. If I didn't get to the bar soon, I would wind up taking a gutter nap in the street. Never an optimal situation in The Nine.

My legs protested, but I pushed them on, pumping them down like limping pistons in a sinking boat. Getting there sooner would be better than later, but later was better than never. I had just about resigned myself to a pace slower than crawling when I heard a crash behind me. I turned my head to see what it was, but all I caught was a stack of rusted pipes rolling on the ground and the shadow of a figure diving into an empty doorway out of sight.

Great. Just what I needed, a greedy tail looking to steal my ride. I pumped my legs harder and stole a glance backward again as I shoved my hand into my jeans pocket and worked out my self-defense surprise. My Knuckle Stunner, a Hellion-born weapon, took brass knuckles to a whole new level. It held a charge that would scramble your brain, and the harder I hit, the thicker the scramble. If this guy thought he could steal my ride, he was in for a noggin rewire he would not soon forget.

Another glance over my shoulder and I caught sight of my pursuer. The thing looked to be about half the size of a man, all hunched, leathery skin with a bulbous head. I didn't need to be able to pick this guy out of a lineup to know one thing for sure. This Hellion was out to ruin my day.

A demon didn't really need an excuse to chase down a Woebegone and tear him apart. I mean, it was Hell. Thing was, they almost always *did* have a reason. I wracked my brain, but as far as I knew, I hadn't given this little cannonball an excuse to hunt me down. I could have slowed down to explain this was a case of mistaken identity, but that would be like hoping a serial killer with a chainsaw would see you're a wonderful person with a sparkling personality and decide not to cleave you in half.

I pumped harder, clutching the Knuckle Stunner in my hand. I could see Hula Harry's less than a block away now. As long as this thing didn't get out into the street and make a desperate sprint, I'd be off my trike and inside before it had a chance to do its Jack the Ripper impression.

When I was within twenty yards, I hopped off and let the tricycle crash into a pile of debris. At this point, if someone wanted the rust basket, they could have it. I ran as hard as I could, heading straight for my salvation. Hula Harry's had an entrance fashioned out of old car doors. All I had to do was get to it, pull the door open, and dive inside ... then maybe bolt it closed for good measure.

My hand reached for the handle, and I felt the cool steel in my palm. Nothing could stop me now. I was home free. That's when I was sideswiped by a seven-hundred-pound linebacker, sweeping my feet clear off the ground.

CHAPTER NINE

Turns out the seven-hundred-pound linebacker wasn't a linebacker at all. It was so much worse. Standing over me was the demon of my nightmares. All leather, shapely skin, and claws. Mastema. She still wore her blindfold, but somehow, I felt her gaze locked on me as I scrambled to get myself into an upright position in the corner of the dark alley where I had landed between the ramshackle buildings. I pressed my back against a corrugated steel wall, half hoping it would give way and let me fall through as Mastema closed the distance between us.

The talons on her feet clacked on the hard ground as she walked. She rolled them upon each footfall as if to increase the creepy effect. The noise was unnerving enough to make Freddie Kruger cringe in his metal glove.

"Sorry, did you want to chat back in Judas's office?" I wanted to sound casual, but my voice came out high and panicked. "You should have said something. We could have grabbed a cup of coffee or a doughnut. This is Hell. There has to be a corner shop somewhere with a horrible musician ..."

Mastema snapped her hand out and shoved it against my mouth, then all but lifted me to my feet by my head. My back was still to the wall, but now I stood on my toes. Mastema leaned in so close the greyed skin of her body brushed against mine. She felt cold and leathery, like a serpent, and I wished I were back in my coffin-sized Agency apartment instead of here getting sized up for the type that fits into a grave.

She looked me up and down for a moment, then pressed a finger from her other hand to her lips to say something along the lines of "shut up or I am going to tear your jaw off and use it as an ashtray." I nodded my compliance, and Mastema let go, spreading her fingers as she pulled her hand away so I could see each of her long, black claws.

She stared at me through that grungy blindfold without moving for a moment, then when she seemed satisfied I wasn't going to assault her with any more of my witty banter, she backed away half a step. She still stood way inside my personal space. The distance of a football field would be too close, but at least it was a start.

"We have business to discuss, you and I."

The sound of her voice made me jump like I'd peed on an electric fence. It was deep, raspy, and not at all human. Something you would imagine a snake might sound like on singles night. It hissed all smooth and inviting and made me want to run away as fast as I could in any direction.

"You can talk?" I squeaked out. Not one of the best opening lines, but I couldn't help but state the obvious. In all the times I had seen her, Mastema had never uttered a single word.

"I mean, that's not to say you shouldn't be able to talk. I just thought because, I don't know, why haven't you ever said anything? I mean, not that you had to, but ..."

Mastema raised her hand again as if to renew her offer to fashion my jaw into a smoking accessory. I beat her to it, slapping my own hand over my mouth.

"Sorry," I said in a muffled voice. "Shutting up."

She paused to look me up and down again, then grinned wide showing rows of sharp, black teeth.

"Better."

I nodded without saying anything else and did everything I could not to recoil from her predatory expression.

"You owe me a debt. I intend to collect on that debt. I want to make the terms of our agreement clear."

My hand fell away from my mouth, and I did my best not to start babbling again. "Debt? No disrespect intended, but I don't remember a debt. Don't get me wrong, what you did to help me fight that big, creepy Hellion clown was incredible and ..."

I stopped myself short of saying I owed her one.

"And I'm sure we would have lost a lot more than Dan's bar had you not come to assist, but I don't remember offering you a debt."

This might sound heartless and ungrateful but owing a demon a genuine debt is no small thing. It's not like buying your buddy pizza and beer when he spends his Saturday afternoon helping you move. This was a demon and owing anything to a demon was like owing your firstborn child to a Great White Shark.

Mastema turned around and tilted her head toward the reddened sky as if she tried to recall something half forgotten.

"You came to the master's office seeking help, did you not? You begged that titanic oaf, Procel, to help you, but he refused in the face of your great need."

"Yes, but ..."

Mastema raised a finger as if to say she was not finished and would not be interrupted.

"You offered him a favor. Anything he wished as long as it was within your power to grant such a favor, correct?"

"Yes, but ..."

Mastema rounded on me again, and I snapped my jaw shut with a clack.

"You said you would have offered the same to anyone brave enough to assist you, but you offered this great gesture to him and still he refused."

I nodded, feeling a lump forming in my throat as I began to follow her reasoning.

"I heeded that call. I came to your aid and slew that face-painted beast. He surely would have destroyed you and turned your mate into his slave."

I coughed. "Alex is not my mate."

"You extended your gesture to anyone who came to your aid." Mastema bit the words off ignoring my comment. "Do you now renounce that agreement?"

"No, I just ..."

"Good," she said, cutting me off again. "Because refusing to honor an agreement to a demon, especially this demon, would have long lasting repercussions."

I slumped back against the wall. She had me dead to rights as far as I could tell. Even if she didn't, there was nothing I could do about it. If Mastema thought I was in her debt, I was, and I would have to repay it, however she saw fit.

"I don't suppose you want Twinkies or maybe a soda?" I let out an uncomfortable laugh. "I've even gone on a Twizzlers run. I can do that for you. Just let me know what you want, and I'll get it for you next time I go Topside."

She let out a giggle which somehow had the same effect as fingernails on a chalkboard. "I don't want your worthless trinkets. I want your services."

A shiver ran up my spine. "What is it you want me to do? Please don't ask me to hurt my friends. I'll do my best to fulfill any request so long as it does not involve any of them."

Mastema's inky lips drew back in an evil grin showing her

predatory teeth again. "I am here simply to solidify the terms of our agreement. When I am ready for you to fulfil your end of our bargain, I will be in touch."

I thought about the way she *touched* me into this alley and hoped it would be none too soon.

"Discretion is important of course," she hissed. "As is your involvement with saving this establishment."

She motioned in the direction of Hula Harry's.

"A desire for privacy is something we both share."

For the first time, I wondered if Mastema had told me the truth. The comments Judas had made in his office made me think he knew about my bar rescue caper, but he never said it outright. Had Mastema kept her part secret? Had Procel blabbed and Judas figured out the rest, or at least had a general idea? I supposed it didn't matter. I owed Mastema, and she intended to collect. This time at least, Judas would have nothing to do with it.

"My lips are sealed."

Mastema nodded. "See that they are, or I can sew them shut in ways that would make you weep for centuries."

I held up my hands in placation. "Whatever visual you are about to burn into my brain, please don't. I get the point. Blab equals unimaginable suffering."

Mastema smiled again. "I see why the master likes you."

I raised an eyebrow. "Like may be a strong word. I think he's learning to tolerate me without too much antacid though."

Mastema let out one of her murderous chuckles, and my spine shared its chill with the rest of my body.

"A word of advice," Mastema said as she slipped away toward the end of the alley. "Don't spend much time out here. Your condition attracts the wrong sort of—" She trailed off. "Just get back to The Agency in one piece. I would like to collect on my debt before you meet any untimely ends."

With that, Mastema launched off the ground in a cloud of rubble and dust as she spread her midnight wings. A single flap of those ebony feathers sent her streaking off across the sky, and I stood alone in the alley wondering what she meant by my condition and more importantly, an untimely end.

CHAPTER TEN

Despite Mastema's ghoulish distraction, I hadn't forgotten about the creature that had followed me to Hula Harry's. Part of me wanted to believe it had been Mastema running me down, but I had gotten a fairly good look at my pursuer. It was small, landbound, and looked nothing like the powerful, shapely build of Mastema. And if it wasn't her, it could still be out there.

With Mastema gone, I was all alone in an alley. I might as well serve myself up on a hotplate with a side of hash browns and a cup of coffee. I sprinted out of the shadows and hurried back to the door of Hula Harry's. A quick glance over my shoulder revealed no other pursuers, so I jerked the door open and went inside.

Hula Harry's was just about the nicest place in The Nine, which might not sound like much considering it was parked in the middle of Hell, but I wouldn't change a thing no matter where it sat. The inside looked much like the exterior. Crushed cars made up the walls, betraying a hood or door here and there that had somehow escaped the destruction to form a sort of impromptu artwork. Working headlights, pointed this way and that, provided ample illumination over the slew of tables and chairs.

Some Woebegone in The Nine deserved to spend an eternity of suffering: murderers, thieves, rapists, child molesters, circus clowns, and IRS accountants. But there were a few, maybe more than a few, who had made a major misstep in life and needed to pay for it but didn't want to keep on living that life of violence or creepy face paint. They were Woebegone like me, and Hula Harry's was a place we could go to be safe without worrying about the dredges of society rushing in to cause trouble.

Of course, Alex and I had a lot to do with that security. Word had gotten around that this place had fallen under the protection of a couple of Judas Agents. That was pretty much all it took to ward off most of the riff raff. I was glad to see there were no exceptions when I wandered up to the bar constructed out of old bus doors and sat down on one of the anti-ergonomic stools.

Dan, Hula Harry's proprietor, sauntered up across from me and offered me a grin. He wore polyester slacks and a canary short sleeve button up, complete with a visible wife-beater underneath. He finished off the ensemble with plastic rimmed glasses, a comb over, and a pipe clenched between his teeth. He glanced down at my gloves and raised an eyebrow at the new fashion accessory.

"What's with the fancy mitts?"

"I took up break dancing and wanted to fit in."

"So, where's your parachute pants and earrings?"

That brought a chuckle to my lips. "You died in the seventies? What do you know about parachute pants?"

"I've seen all types in here. Saggy pants, red leather jackets, bell bottom jeans, all the idiots make a showing sooner or later."

I laughed again. "Give me a shot of the good stuff."

Dan pulled a can of Coca-Cola out from under the bar along with a glass, popped the top, and poured. Here at Hula Harry's, the good stuff had nothing to do with thirty-year-old scotch or a high dollar tequila. It was all about the sugary goodness of soda. Sure, he had booze. Pretty much every type known to man lined the shelves at the back of the bar, but it didn't do any good. Alcohol didn't have the kick it did Topside. We were in Hell. Having booze that worked would be like a free vacation to Disneyland. Instead, we got to enjoy something much rarer. Sugary, caffeine-filled soda. I had set up Dan with a black-market pipeline to a Topside supplier, and now he had the only place in town where you could crack open a cold one. He did a decent business, and in turn, offered a little bit of normalcy to an otherwise horrific existence. It was a win-win all around, and I got to drink for free whenever I came by. I couldn't ask for much else.

I glanced over my shoulder at the door and scanned the bar, surveying the crowd. There were quite a few Woebegone in attendance. Almost every one of Dan's mismatched steel and iron tables were occupied with patrons enjoying conversation and soda. I couldn't help but continue to check my back for the thing that had followed me all the way to the bar.

"You expecting someone?" Dan poured the last of the can into my glass as the foam settled down, and he tossed the can into the trash.

"Something weird tailed me here. I'm a little worried it will barge in and ruin your ambiance, that's all."

"Don't worry about me. I swear, ever since you did battle with that demon outside, business has never been better. It's like they want to see a little trouble brewing up in here."

I chuckled and took a drink. "Well, I'd be happy to see a nice, peaceful evening without any demon battles."

"You and me both." Dan huffed. "And don't worry about that thing outside. It was probably some creep looking for trouble. I'll bet he got bored and took off as soon as you walked in here."

I nodded, even though I wasn't all that sure Dan was right. The thing that had followed me wasn't some Woebegone out for a dust up. It had been a demon. And what did Mastema mean about getting back to The Agency before I ran into trouble? Could my new malady be some sort of demon pheromone? That would be all I needed. A bunch of horny imps chasing me around the underworld like teenage boys at the prom. I would never live that one down.

A tap on my shoulder sent me spinning, and I raised an arm ready to ward off any unwanted demon affection.

"Whoa, take it easy." Jazzy stood behind me with Meg, both of them retreating a step at my sudden defensive posture. "We just came over to say hi, not mug you."

Dan let out a little laugh under his breath and nodded to the girls. "Can I get you anything?"

"No, we're good." Jazzy lifted a glass to show him she still had a full soda in her hand.

"All right. Let me know. I'm going to go make my rounds." Dan retreated and started making his way around the tables picking up glasses and taking orders. I dropped my arm and turned the rest of the way around to face Meg and Jazzy.

"Sorry about that. I guess I'm a little on edge. How are things?"

Jazzy and Meg were an inseparable duo and mutual friends of Zoe, a woman who meant the world to me. I had saved Zoe from the cruelty of The Nine. I had also failed her, and she had run off to pursue her own brand of vigilante violence somewhere in The Nine. I hadn't seen her since. Jazzy and Meg always reminded me that Zoe was still out there somewhere.

"Good," Jazzy said. She was a Latina fitness freak who could give most bouncers a run for their money. "We're keeping the shop up and running for you. People ask how you're doing all the time."

Before joining The Judas Agency, I had kept myself busy by running a little black-market shop of my own. When I had gotten recruited, Zoe had taken the place over, and now Meg and Jazzy had done a great job with it since she'd been gone.

"Why don't you come by and say hello?" Meg, Jazzy's counterpart with the ivory skin and fire engine red hair, wasn't as buff as Jazzy, but she always kept herself decked out in black leather which lent to a similar badassery appearance. "I promise we won't bite—much."

I let out a laugh, and my eyes went to the floor. I wanted to ask them about Zoe, if they had seen or heard from her. I resisted the urge to sound like a broken record, but the longer the silence stretched between us the louder the unspoken question seemed to become.

"We haven't heard anything." Jazzy finally said, reaching out to put a hand on my shoulder. "I swear, even if she asks us not to, we'll tell you if she shows up again."

I looked up at the two of them again and reached up to cover Jazzy's hand with my own. "Thanks, that means a lot."

"Of course, Zoe will have our hides for going behind her back." Meg finished. "So, you will owe us a big one."

She shot me a wink, and I nodded a tight-lipped grin back at her.

Dan came up behind us and broke the awkward atmosphere. "You three up for an adventure?"

My back was to the bar, so I didn't know what Dan carried, but the expression on Jazzy and Meg's faces twisted into a mixture of fear and dread. Fearing the worst, I turned around to see what Dan was talking about.

He carried three shot glasses in his hands, all bearing a bright blue liquid of some sort.

"Not again," Meg whined. "Can't you find someone else to

be your guinea pigs? Last time I drank one of your creations, I peed green for a week."

"Sorry about that." Dan offered a sheepish grin. "It was a flaw in the formulation. This one is different, I promise. It's a winner for sure. Just try it, you'll see."

I gave him a look and then eyed the shot glasses. "I don't know, Dan. Meg's right. Your concoctions can be a little ... volatile."

Dan deflated a few inches. "How am I supposed to find a signature drink for Hula Harry's if no one will try my proto-types? It's not my fault that booze won't work down here. I need something that can wow the customer base, even without the ninety-proof kick. That requires some creative concocting."

Dan clasped his hands together and hit the three of us with his best puppy dog eyes.

The toughest one caved first.

"Fine." Jazzy reached out for a shot glass and held it in front of her chest. "But if my tongue turns orange or my head explodes, I am coming back to haunt you."

She shifted her gaze to the two of us and lifted an eyebrow. "I hope you don't think I'm doing this alone."

After a half a beat of silence, I reached out for one of the shot glasses, and Meg did the same.

"Here's to new flavors and crazy adventures." I raised my glass, and the others followed suit, clinking mine with their own, then all three of us threw the shot back at the same time.

The flavor was sweet at first. Sort of a cotton candy that had been sitting in the sun for too long. That's when the afterburn kicked in. It wasn't the fire of a stiff bourbon or scotch; this was the fire of the unholy union between a habanero and a ghost pepper. My eyes began to water, and my throat threatened to close up. Both of my hands went to my neck as I croaked out the word.

"Drink!"

Dan pulled out three sodas, and the three of us jerked them away, opened them ourselves, and up-ended the cans over our mouths.

Dan's face never lost its toothy grin while he waited for us to finish dousing the flames.

"What do you think?" He finally asked when the three of us had slowed our panting to more of a rapid wheeze. "I call it Candy Caliente."

"More like Diabetic Pepper Spray." Meg took another swig of her soda. "That's worse than the last one."

Dan's shoulders fell, and he swept the glasses off the counter. "I'm trying to create something no one has ever experienced before."

"Mission accomplished," I said. "Although I have never experienced a firehose colostomy either, and it's not something I would add to my bucket list."

Meg laughed and pressed a finger to her nose to say I was spot on.

"Maybe you should shoot for something more pleasurable than shocking." Meg set her empty can on the bar and shrugged. "You know the old saying about bees and honey."

Dan nodded, and I could already see his wheels turning. "Thanks, I think I might have a few ideas. Why don't you three stick around for a little while?"

With that, Dan headed to the other end of the bar, pulled out a large mixer, and began compiling ingredients on the counter.

I turned to Meg and smiled. "You just created a monster."

"Yeah," Jazzy said. "And I am not going to stick around for him to finish his evil potion. My stomach can barely handle one, much less two."

I nodded. "I think it would be best if we slipped out while he's preoccupied."

Truth was, I felt pretty exhausted anyway. This overuse sickness took its toll, and I still had a long ride back to The Agency, assuming my little demon friend wasn't waiting outside for me.

We waited for Dan to turn his back for more ingredients then all three of us tip-toed toward the door and slipped out, leaving the patrons of Hula Harry's as victims to Dan's new concoctions.

CHAPTER ELEVEN

I made it back to The Judas Agency in one exhausted piece. Whatever had tracked me to Hula Harry's got bored or decided I wasn't worth the trouble. Either way, my pint-sized pursuer had moved on to greener pastures, and I was happy to see it go.

I stood in front of a mirror in the apartment locker room. It was a community space for the residents to clean up, change, store their belongings, pretty much everything we couldn't do in our so-called apartments. Judas Agents were issued more of a sleeping coffin with just enough room to slide in and rest. Don't get me wrong, ever since I had started staying here, I'd slept like a baby. Who wouldn't? It was safe, secure, and comfortable. Nothing like the wastelands outside where every serial rapist, murderer, and Mary Kay Commando could come bang on your door. My apartment was small, but I slept in the comfort of knowing only Agency murderers surrounded me.

I stared at my reflection and gazed into my own dark eyes. They were cradled in shadowy bags, bloodshot and clouded with exhaustion. All in all, I looked half-starved and sleep deprived. Standing there in a t-shirt and sweatpants only emphasized my need for rest.

I scooped my things off the shelf in front of me and piled them all into my open locker. When I turned around again, a familiar face appeared in the doorway to the room.

Barry, or Bear as he was affectionately called, was a mountain of a man. Dark skin, shoulders wide enough to fill a walk-in closet, and enough body hair to make an afghan jealous.

"Gabe." His deep baritone voice all but shook the room in greeting. "Haven't seen you around much. How've you been?"

He took up a post at a sink next to me and began stacking his own toiletries along the edge.

"I've been pretty good. A little tired. Looking forward to getting some rest tonight. I hope you're not planning to snore too much."

Bear rumbled out a laugh. "No promises, but I'll do my best."

I reached out to grab the rest of my stuff and realized I didn't have my gloves on. My hands weren't any better. In fact, they looked like they had seen a month in the desert after a weed whacker manicure. Bear saw them too. His eyes flicked over to my hands then up to my eyes for the smallest moment before they went back to studying his own face in the mirror.

I cursed myself for being so careless and shoved the rest of my belongings into my locker and slammed it shut. I was just about to hurry out the door when Bear stopped me.

"Hold up a second, Gabe."

He retreated from his mirror and walked in my direction. For a moment, I thought he might ask for another look at my hands, but he passed me by, peering around the corner to be sure we were alone.

"Seems like you've run into a little trouble after all."

I put my hands behind my back to keep them out of sight

and shrugged. "Looks way worse than it is. A little Oil of Olay and they'll be supple as a baby's butt."

I started to walk away, but Bear clamped one of his huge hands down on my shoulder. It was like having a truck fall on my arm and then drag me back.

"Listen," he said, turning me back around to face him. "I may not be the sharpest tool in the shed, but that's no small problem. I've seen it before. Not quite that bad, but I know one thing for sure. There's no cure for it here in The Nine. Use all the lotion you want, that's not going away, and your hands are only the beginning."

My eyebrows knitted together as I peered up into Bear's serious face. "No offense, but everything you just said brings up more questions than answers. How do you know about this? What do you mean there's no cure, and could you please let go of me? You are breaking my shoulder."

Bear let out a chuckle and took his hand off me. "Sorry, sometimes I don't know my own strength."

"Well, it's considerable." I reached up to rub my aching joint, before realizing I had exposed my hands again. I really needed to put my gloves back on.

"And I said there's no cure in The Nine." Bear held up a finger and retreated to his own locker for a moment then came back with a business card. "As Agents, we have the unique opportunity to search out help in other places."

I glanced down at the card and then my eyes shot back up to Bear again.

"No."

Bear shrugged. "Say what you will, she knows more than anyone down here about your illness. I've seen her work a miracle or two myself. She might be able to help you. I would go sooner rather than later though. If that issue gets any worse, you might not make it up to see her at all."

I studied the card in my hand. It said Medjine Dasmy,

Voodoo Arts and Witch Doctor. The address at the bottom looked all too familiar.

"Alex is not going to be happy about this one," I said under my breath.

"What's that?" Bear asked.

"Nothing. Thank you for the advice. I'll check it out."

Bear nodded and headed back to his sink. "Go get some rest. You'll need it if you're going to see her in the morning."

CHAPTER TWELVE

Alex's cubicle resided in a sea of grey misery usually reserved only for prisons and school cafeterias. Every time I came to this floor, I was amazed at the sheer expanse of workspace desolation. The space inside far exceeded the exterior dimensions of the building, offering the sensation of being lost in a vast desert—if it were made of grey fabric and industrial carpeting.

"Good morning." I rounded the corner to Alex's slice of cubicle depression and saw her working away at her computer. I had died in the eighties, so computers weren't much of a thing for me, but Alex always said The Judas Agency's network surpassed anything the Topside techs could muster. Something about privacy laws and something called a fiery wall. It was all gibberish to me. I just knew if there was a needle to be found, Alex knew which haystack to dive into.

She raised her hand and made a pinching motion with her fingers, a gesture meant to close the window according to the rudimentary education I had received on the thing. I had a cubicle and a computer too, but I believed in good old-fashioned footwork. There was no substitute for a well-placed informant. Besides, sitting in one of these suicide inducers all day would be enough to make me want to crawl into a corner and never come out again.

As soon as the window shut down, Alex spun her chair to face me. Judging from the furrowed expression on her face, the haystack had come out on the winning side today.

"What's up? Your spy T.V. on strike?"

Alex sneered. "Your spy T.V. on strike?" She mocked me in a squeaky tone meant to approximate my voice. It was in no way accurate.

I held up my hands and leaned back on my heels. "Take it easy. I can come back when you're feeling a little less stabby, if you like."

"Sorry." Alex let out a breath. "You just caught me at a bad time. I did a little recon on our operation yesterday. Turns out it was a total flop."

I stepped into her cubicle and leaned against one of the padded grey walls. "Well, you pretty much told them we were complete frauds, so I'm not sure why you're surprised."

Alex narrowed her eyes at me in a way that had me thinking I should have stayed out in the walkway.

"The only reason I had to make up that story was because you passed out in the middle of the sidewalk."

"And I can't tell you how much I appreciate that amazing story."

Alex kept staring at me.

"... or how much the entire thing was my fault."

That drew a nod from Alex, and she turned back to her computer while I rolled my eyes. Not where she could see me, of course. I wanted to keep my eyeballs right where they were.

"I pulled up this cell phone audio of a meeting they had with one of the leaders that night. Listen to this."

"... it's just like she said."

I recognized the voice. It was Gold Cap from the street.

"They're trying to play us against each other. They want us fighting, so they can keep us under their thumb."

My eyes went wide at the crackly transmission.

"How could they know we were—"

Alex held up a hand. "Hold on a second, just listen."

Rustling fabric obscured some of the chatter, but then the voices got clear again.

"Why would the government barge into our business? They could care less about us."

Another voice, this one deeper and more grizzled. "Because we're getting too strong. We're making our mark, and they don't like it. The suits think they can start a war. If it's a war they want, it's a war they're going to get."

"They think some government organization hired us?" I whispered and continued to listen to the conversation.

Alex shrugged. "We told him some guy in a suit hired us. I guess they took it literally. Check out this next part."

"So, what are we going to do about it?" Gold Cap said.

"We're going to take this to Marcella and see what she has to say."

Gold Cap groaned his disapproval.

"Listen up. Marcella brought us all together and showed us how the suits turn us against each other. She deserves your respect, and you will give it to her."

"She has my respect, but we can handle this. Why don't we just—"

There was the sound of a struggle and muffled voices, this time they sounded loud and angry, but they were no longer discernible. Alex let the recording go for a few more seconds and then waved a hand in front of the screen. The audio paused, and Alex turned back to me again.

"It pretty much goes on like that until he leaves. The phone must have fallen further into his pocket or something, but you get the gist of the conversation."

I folded my arms and nodded. "Who is this Marcella woman? Have you ever heard of her?"

Alex shook her head. "I did a search, and nothing came up."

When I didn't respond, Alex leaned in and caught my gaze.

"Did you hear me? The Judas Agency network pulled up nothing. That does not happen. Our network knows the history of every soul, living or dead, on the planet. This Marcella does not exist, or she's a ghost—which would show up in our system too."

I shrugged. "So, what can we do about it? If we don't know who she is, how can we work against her?"

"We're just going to have to up our game. Throw a grenade they can't ignore."

"I think grenades are pretty hard to ignore," I said. "Of course, everyone's too dead to get the message. Maybe we should go with something a little more subtle, like a brick through the window. We could write a note in magazine clippings all serial killer style. It'll be fun. Like arts and crafts."

Alex brought her eyes down to me again and focused on my face. "What are you talking about? Are you feeling sick again?"

"No, I'm fine." I smiled. "I feel a hundred percent better. This is just a passing phase. I'll be good as new in a few days."

Alex nodded then reached out to snatch my arm faster than a coked-up ninja. "Let me see your hands."

Before I could resist, she had unfastened the Velcro backing and yanked my glove off. As soon as she saw the state of my skin, she recoiled and let go.

"Gabe, this is not better. It's way worse."

I peered down at the cracked skin on my hands. They had gone from chapped lines to oozing fissures, and the condition was beginning to make its way up to my wrists as well.

I sighed and turned my hand over, exposing my palm which looked equally as bad. "I guess it is a little worse. The cracking seems to be spreading to my feet and knees too."

I glanced at Alex and looked away just as fast. I knew it was bad but knowing it and seeing her reaction were two different things. The alarm on her face made the whole thing all too real.

"I do feel better." I pulled my glove back on to hide my hand from view. "A good night's sleep was just what I needed."

Alex stood, put her hands on my cheeks and forced me to look her in the eye.

"No amount of sleep is going to fix this." She squeezed my face harder. "Do you understand?"

I tried to nod, but her hands locked my head in place, holding my gaze.

"Yes, I understand."

She stared at me for a long moment then let go. I resisted the urge to rub my jaw as she retreated a few inches and leaned against her desk.

"I did a little more digging and a condition as advanced as yours is bad. Overusing your Topside power causes cracks in ..." She paused trying to come up with the right word.

"It sort of cracks your shell. The thing that houses your soul."

"I have cracks in my soul?" I eyed her with suspicion.

She punched me in the arm and shook her head. "This is serious. Not in your soul, the part that holds it in. Think of it like a dam. It keeps leaking until the cracks get so big the whole thing gives way."

I looked at her no longer feeling quite so clever. "And then what happens?"

Alex shrugged. "It was hard for me to find out even that much. We can't die, but without a soul, you don't really exist either. I have no idea what will happen. And there's no..."

She trailed off, not wanting to finish the sentence, so I finished it for her.

"No cure."

I let the words hang for a moment then pulled the card Bear had given me out of my back pocket.

"No cure in The Nine, at least."

Alex peered down at the card, and her eyes flicked back up to me.

"You've got to be kidding."

I tilted my head and took the card back. "No one said an incurable disease would be easy. I'll go alone, if you don't want to come."

Alex punched me again, this time hard enough to make me stagger back a step.

"If you think you're going up there alone, you have another thing coming. Let's get changed. We don't have any time to lose."

CHAPTER THIRTEEN

"Looks like the place is closed." Alex rapped her knuckles on the old sliding steel door. Medjine Dasmy's Voodoo shop was located in an unlikely alley in the middle of Denver, Colorado. I would have expected her to own a shop in New Orleans or even Florida. I never thought to ask why she chose the Mile High City the last time we had met. To be honest, Alex and I had been too freaked out by the encounter to ask much of anything. Medjine Dasmy was a little—let's just call her intense. That and Alex liked dark magic about as much a leech facial.

"Maybe she went out to lunch," I said. "We could go check out a few sights then come back and—"

Before I finished, the sliding metal door slammed open so hard Alex and I jumped back ready for a fight. In the doorway stood a familiar looking woman with dark skin and her usual full length white-laced dress. Her impressive girth took up most of the opening, and she appraised us with her bulging, blood-shot brown eyes. If she had noticed the fact that Alex and I were ready to do battle, she didn't show it. She just hurried out the door, grabbed me by the collar, and threw me into the shop like a kid who had stayed out way past their curfew.

"Get inside, fool. You are leaking all over the street."

Medjine reached for Alex as well, but she hurried into the shop before the big woman could manhandle her too.

Together, we watched as Medjine grabbed a large pot off a shelf near the door then threw off the top and began casting the powdered contents into the alley outside the shop. She went as far as the street then hurried back, replaced the empty pot on the shelf, then retrieved a box of wooden matches.

"You may want to shield your eyes."

She struck the match and dropped it onto the alley, and everything flashed into a powder keg of light and smoke. The noise wasn't all that loud, but I felt the whump in my chest. Judging from the multitude of car alarms now going off in the street, they felt it out there too.

Medjine reached up and slammed her door shut then secured it with a piece of rebar before turning back to us.

"What are you two doing back in my shop? I offer to help, and you bring me trouble. Is that it?"

I shook my head, and Alex held out her hands. Her eyes darted everywhere, and I could tell she was not handling the fact that she was locked inside of a Voodoo shop very well.

"I don't know what you're talking about." I took a small step toward Medjine but didn't go any farther. "We aren't here to cause any trouble. We just want to talk. I have a bit of a problem and ... well, you probably aren't going to believe this, but Alex and I aren't what we seem."

Medjine eyed me for a minute and huffed out a laugh. "So, you aren't Agents of the underworld come to wreak havoc among the living? What are you then, a couple of skunks?"

I stood there with my mouth half open and looked over at Alex. She had gone still as well.

"You arrogant 'Begones all think you know so much just

because you've been wandering down below for a few years. You weren't smart enough to use the bath powder I prescribed for you last time you were here, Mr. Gabriel." She shot me a disgusted look and put her hands on her hips to emphasize the scolding. "If you had, your soul wouldn't be leaking out all over my floor." Her stare bore into me until I had to look away.

The last time we had visited, Medjine offered me a tin of nondescript powder and told me to take a bath in it. I thought she was off her rocker and had thrown the tin in the nearest dumpster. Maybe I should have paid more attention to her magic bath salts.

"Sorry, I guess I am a little behind. You know what we are and what's wrong with me?"

Medjine rolled her soul piercing eyes and scooted past me in the aisle, tiptoeing over some unseen substance on the floor.

"Only the blind could miss something this bad, child." She grabbed a towel and threw it on the floor next to my feet. "You mind standing on that, please?"

I chuckled a little, thinking she was kidding. But when she fixed her stare on me again, I decided to step onto the towel.

"You must have every low-level demon in The Nine tracking you. Do you know what they would give for a chance to lap up a soul like yours? It would mean no small amount of power. It's a good thing their boss has such an intolerant view of soul skimming or you would already be a demon buffet."

I thought about the creature who had tracked me to Hula Harry's and wondered what would have happened if it had caught me.

"A friend sent me here and said you might be able to help. Is there anything I can do to stop this from getting worse?"

"Yes, there was something, but you were too smart and threw it away. You cast the cure of a crazy old woman into a dumpster, and now that no one else can help, you're back looking for a miracle."

"Listen," Alex piped in. "Last time we were here, you played up the crazy Voodoo bit. We had no idea you wanted to help or even that something was wrong. You never told us what that stuff was for, you just told him to dive in. For all we knew, that tin contained poison bath salts or powdered acid."

Medjine glared at Alex for a moment then backed down a notch or two. "Maybe I could have been clearer in my diagnosis, but you should not be so quick to dismiss the power of my religion."

Alex let out a little laugh. "Believe me, we are the last ones to dismiss anything after some of the stuff we've seen."

It occurred to me that Medjine might have an idea about how to get Simeon out of Ryan's body as well. After all, she did seem to specialize in displaced souls.

"Since we're on the subject, do you know anything about possessions? I only ask because we have a friend who's sort of stuck in his body with another spirit and—"

Medjine held up a hand to interrupt, leaving me with my mouth half open as she walked over to look me up and down. She squeezed my arm, lifted my hand and sniffed my armpit, then winced back, crinkling her nose. "Your friend should be the least of your worries. I have never seen a spirit shell this broken. The true miracle is that you have any soul left at all."

I snapped my mouth shut, drawn in by the gravity of her words.

"What happens if my soul ... if I can't keep my soul from disappearing?" I swallowed, hoping to push down the fear knot rising in my throat. Alex had taken to kneading her hands in front of her chest, and I could tell she battled a knot of her own.

Medjine shook her head. "It is a fate much worse than the one dealt to you already. With no soul, you are empty in a way that is almost impossible to describe."

She paused for a moment to think then looked up at me.

"Have you ever lost anyone close to you? Had a stranger tell you that someone you love was gone forever?"

I nodded, feeling my chest go heavy at the mere thought.

"Do you remember the cold emptiness in your heart at that instant? That sensation that something had been torn away from you, leaving you unwhole and full of sorrow? That endless sense of falling and darkness. That moment—that agony—is what you will experience for the rest of eternity ... but you will not know why. You will exist as an empty husk, endlessly searching for that thing you lost but can't remember. You will wander your realm in agonizing sorrow forever."

I stared down into Medjine's eyes. They were full of empathy and sadness, and I knew the answer to my next question before I asked it.

"Is there anything you can do to stop it?"

"No." Her answer came out in a near whisper, and the single word cut me like a knife.

Alex choked out a sob as she put her hands up over her mouth. Tears threatened to overrun her eyes.

I took a breath and let it out, ready to thank Medjine for her help when she reached up and tapped the locket hidden under my shirt.

"But there is something you can do."

CHAPTER FOURTEEN

I backed away out of instinct, covering the locket hidden beneath my shirt with my hand. Medjine offered a crooked smile and let her arm fall without pursuing and didn't say anything else.

"It's just a family heirloom. It doesn't do anything." I tried to sound convincing.

When Medjine's face began to twist back into that familiar expression of indignant anger, Alex stepped up behind me and put a hand on my shoulder. "I think we all know that's not just a piece of junk jewelry. We came here looking for a cure, and Tylenol isn't going to do the trick. Why don't you come clean about the locket?"

I dropped my hand and let out a sigh.

"Sorry, I guess it's a reflex when you live—well, you know."

Medjine's face softened a little, and she tilted her head. "Where did you come by that item?"

"A Woebegone woman came to me looking to get rid of it. She said some bad people were after the power it held, and she didn't want the responsibility anymore. I checked out her story and wound up working a trade. I've kept the locket hidden ever since."

There was a little more to that tale, but I decided to keep the more unscrupulous parts of my younger years to myself.

"And have you ever learned what your prize can do?"

Her question sparked a flame of hope somewhere deep inside me. Could this woman decipherer the Origin Artifact? Could she tell us what my locket would do if we activated it? The implications of having such an answer seemed almost unthinkable.

"No," I said. "I suspect it's powerful, but I've only held it. I have no idea how to use an item like this or what it might do."

Medjine nodded and stepped closer to me again. "May I see it?"

I pulled the locket out from under my shirt and let it fall against my chest. I was willing to let her see it but couldn't bring myself to remove the precious item and lay it in her hands. She eyed me for a moment then her mouth quirked in a crooked smile again as she leaned in close.

She squinted at the aged detail of the piece but did not reach out to touch it.

"Yes, this item has great power. It is like trying to decipher light by staring into the sun. It is too bright, too powerful, but I can sense its rudimentary purpose."

I nodded, feeling my eyes go wide with expectation. Even Alex leaned forward with anticipation.

"The locket—" She paused for a moment as if trying to choose her words. "It is not so much a healing implement, but it can be used in such a fashion. It links two entities as one, forcing them to work in a sort of symbiotic harmony ... or disharmony."

My shoulders sank in disappointment. I had always thought of an Origin Artifact as something that could unleash cataclysmic harm or even good. A cosmic set of handcuffs hardly lived up to the hype.

"I don't understand. How is that supposed to help me?"

"There is only one way in which to repair your shell, and that is to fuse it with another. Bonding yourself—your shell—to another living being will heal you and make you whole once again."

Alex stepped forward and raised a hand. "I'll do it. Whatever I have to do, if it will help, I'm in."

My eyes went up to meet Alex's hopeful gaze. Her willingness to sacrifice anything to help me tied a knot in my stomach. Tears tried to break through to the surface, but I forced them back down, not wanting to put such a blatant expression of emotion on display.

Medjine smiled and reached for Alex's hand. "I'm afraid you won't do. It has to be a living being, and that is one thing you are not able to offer."

The deflated expression on Alex's face brought a whole new set of emotions I had to tamp down.

"Thank you for the offer." I smiled. "We can be soulmates some other time, I promise."

Alex choked out a laugh and nodded, then she turned her attention back to Medjine. "So, what do you mean, join with another living being? How does that work?"

Medjine let go of Alex's hand and turned back to me. "It's just as it sounds. Once joined, you will be forever connected to that being. You know the advantage, of course, but there are disadvantages as well."

"Whatever the being, you will need to maintain a physical connection with it. The smaller and less intelligent the animal is, the less time you will be able to withstand being away. A human is best. I suspect you could be separated for up to a week without suffering any effects. Something like a rabbit or a mouse might be as short as a few minutes. A dog would be somewhere in between."

"What about a cat? They are pretty smart."

Medjine shook her head in short, little jerks. "Do not bond with a feline. They walk the line between the living and the dead already. You would wind up serving it rather than the other way around."

Alex laughed. "No cats. The real question is where are we going to find a person willing to join with you? Seems like a big sacrifice. And what happens when they die? Do they have a guaranteed ticket to The Nine?"

Medjine shrugged. "I don't see where willingness should have much of a say in who you join with. As for what happens in the afterlife, you would know better than me. I can only give you the roadmap. How you get there and what happens when you arrive is up to you."

I nodded. "So how do we make it work?"

Medjine squinted at the worn silver again as if she were trying to read some sort of fine script printed on the outside.

"I'm not sure. Many times, knowing its purpose is enough. Simply willing the item with enough conviction could activate it."

I sighed. "So, all we have to do is find some guy willing to bind his soul to mine, then imagine my locket to life in order to save me from an eternity of sorrow. Sounds easy."

Medjine narrowed her eyes at me. "If you wanted the easy way, you should have taken that bath."

I chuckled and nodded. "Believe me, next time a strange woman invites me to take a bath, I'll be all over it."

CHAPTER FIFTEEN

"How about this guy?" Alex pointed to a jogger in short shorts, a t-shirt, and mirrored sunglasses.

"I would rather go on as a soulless husk for the rest of eternity."

We had left Medjine's Voodoo shop almost an hour ago and had been wondering the city sidewalks ever since. We made our way to a park that seemed to have a larger population of ducks than people and decided to circle the small lake path while we talked through my soulmate options.

I still felt terrible that we hadn't gotten any information that could help Ryan. Right now, I felt like Medjine was our best hope at finding a way to dislodge Simeon, but I needed to solve my problems first. I couldn't help Ryan as an underworld zombie. Once we had my leakage issues sorted out, Medjine would be my first stop, and I would do whatever it took to convince her to help us save our friend.

"Aw, come on," Alex chided. "At least choose someone who's easy on the eyes. If I have to look at him all the time, I'd like to enjoy the view."

My eyebrows went up. "Who said I planned to choose a him?"

I glanced across the vast expanse of grass and bike paths and spotted a woman in a bikini top playing Frisbee with her dog on the far side of the park.

Alex held up a finger in front of my face. "Don't say it."

I let out a little chuckle. "You said easy on the eyes. I was just trying to accommodate."

Alex gave me a little jab to the midsection. "Fine. We are looking for a homely person with a likeable personality. That shouldn't be too hard to find."

"Said every unmarried male or female on the planet."

"I've known a few married people who said it too." Alex laughed.

"We should definitely find someone in good shape. I wouldn't mind taking a shortcut to six pack abs and biceps the size of watermelons."

"Medjine said symbiotic not synergistic. You aren't going to gain some sort of wonder twin powers. If this turns you into a superhero, I'll be in line right behind you."

"All joking aside." I turned my gaze to Alex and fixed her with a serious stare. "I'm not sure I can curse some innocent into being my surrogate soul cage. Even Medjine wasn't sure how it would affect them in the long run. I could be damning a good person to an eternity in The Nine for no reason. Not to mention the fact that I would be physically connected to that person for the rest of their lives, maybe longer."

"So, what's the alternative?" Alex threw out her hands in frustration. "Bind with a dog or some other animal that would have to remain connected at your hip? At least with a human, it's possible to be separated for a reasonable length of time. You could pop up for a visit once a week, get your soul fix or whatever it is you need, and then you can both go about your business."

I sighed. "I would feel more comfortable if someone did it willingly."

Alex groaned out an affirmation but didn't say much else.

"Tell you what," she said, after walking a few minutes in silence. "I'm going over there to grab us a couple of ice cream cones." She pointed across the park to a cart where a guy in a red and white striped apron stood under an umbrella. "While I'm gone, you think of a list of super friendly people who would want to donate their everlasting life to you."

Before I could say anything, Alex smacked me on the shoulder a couple of times for encouragement then ran off, leaving me alone with my thoughts.

She was right. Why would anyone in their right minds sacrifice their soul to save mine? It was a ludicrous idea. I would either have to find someone to use against their will or find the world's smartest animal. Maybe I could join with a porpoise. They are supposed to be ultra-intelligent. There would be the whole water issue, but I could find one at SeaWorld or something. That wouldn't be so bad. I could come back every few days and bring it a fish or two. Plus, they're as big as a human or even bigger. Medjine said that size mattered as well. It seemed just crazy enough to work.

I turned to see that Alex was still standing at the ice cream cart. She pointed into the cart at something, presumably choosing which flavor she wanted. I hoped they had Rocky Road.

I stepped off the path and meandered toward a bench next to the lake. It would be a nice place to relax and a fitting spot to tell Alex about my porpoise idea. I was about to sit down when a movement caught my eye in a stand of trees to my right. I squinted into the shadows and saw that someone stood among the greenery. Much to my surprise, Sammy waved her arms over her head as if to gain my attention. The moment I spotted her, she pointed behind me. I wasn't sure what she could be pointing at, other than Alex at the ice cream cart, but I looked over my shoulder anyway.

I caught my breath as I realized something was very wrong. The landscape seemed out of place or unnatural, but I couldn't put my finger on why. It wasn't anything overt, but a tiny voice inside me screamed to get out of its way.

I continued to scan the open grass and pathway, looking for the anomaly. Not even an unfriendly spider jumped onto my radar. Then I saw it. A shimmer in the light, almost indistinguishable from its surroundings. Like a reflection off of sand, it just shouldn't be there.

The moment I laid eyes on it, the shimmer began to move. Worse, it headed straight for me. The strange anomaly crept slowly at first, like a cat stalking its prey, then all at once, it shot forward in a burst of speed. The shimmer bounded twice, and it was on top of me. I felt the sensation of my body breaking some sort of barrier, then my surroundings went all blurry. But that was the least of my worries.

I was now on my back fighting off a three-foot-tall mound of muscle and leathery skin. I recognized its bulbous head, spindly hair, dark eyes, and sharp teeth. It was the demon who had tracked me to Hula Harry's. My stomach lurched, causing my heart rate to jump to hummingbird speed. I couldn't believe he had followed me Topside. Even the thought of a demon hopping up to the land of the living without permission was enough to get it boiled in his own body fluids. Medjine was right. If this thing had chased me all the way up here, he must be desperate to steal whatever soul I had left.

Panic surged through me as the little demon sat on my chest, crushing the air out of my lungs. He was short, but he must have weighed three hundred pounds. I flailed my arms and legs, trying to force him off, but he managed to hold me down, pressing one hand into my face while he fought to capture one of my thrashing hands. When he did, he jerked my arm hard enough to pop my shoulder out of its socket and shoved my fingers into his drooling mouth.

He sunk his teeth into my flesh, holding my hand in place. The pain made me call out in agony, but I had no air with which to scream. My body became heavy. I felt like I had been drugged, and all I could do was lay there. A strange sensation coursed through me. As if a pump had been installed to syphon off my blood—except it wasn't blood. My spirit drained away, emptying me of something precious, weakening me with every second.

Why wouldn't anyone help? A demon had appeared in broad daylight, and no one had so much as screamed. Then I noticed my surroundings again. They were all blurred and off color. The demon had us inside of some sort of camouflage. From the outside, we would look like nothing more than the vague shimmer I had seen bounding across the grass. We were all but invisible. My heart pounded in my chest as I tried to get my breathing and thoughts under control. If I couldn't find a way to bring the shield down, Alex wouldn't find me until it was too late.

I gathered what strength I had left and used my free hand to search the demon's waist, then its arm and wrist. That's when I found it. A Hellion shield generator of some kind. I clawed at it, got my fingers under the band, and then yanked. The generator came free and fell into the grass at my side. I reached for it, but the demon was faster. He snatched it out of my grasp, grinning around the drooling, bloody mess of my fingers.

I was all but limp now, and the demon grabbed my other hand, lifting it to shove into his mouth with the other. He bit down and sucked harder. I let out a soundless scream, but it was no use. I wanted to retch, but I didn't have the strength. I could only turn my head side to side and beg him to stop. But he wouldn't. This lowly Hellion was devouring the meal of his life, and he planned to enjoy every last drop. I would be left an empty husk, and this demon would be more powerful than he ever had a right to be.

My arms were lifeless in his grasp now as the darkness began to take me. I looked for any sign of Alex. Hadn't Sammy been there too? Maybe she would help. Maybe she would point Alex to my rescue.

The last of my spirit rose into my shoulders ... the last of myself. This creature had defiled me in a way I could not have imagined. I would never be the same. My eyes became heavy, and I knew it was over. No one could stop it now.

No one except a charging Voodoo princess screaming across the park like a warrior queen.

CHAPTER SIXTEEN

"Don't try to get up." Alex's voice came out of the fog as the world rematerialized around me. I squinted at the sky, seeing first a blue so bright it hurt my eyes, then I gave a weak smile as the form of my partner crouching over me came into focus. She wore an expression so full of concern I wanted to sit up and tell her it was all right.

When I tried to do just that, she put a gentle hand on my chest to hold me down.

"Relax," she said in a soothing voice. "Let Medjine finish her work."

The mere mention of the Voodoo princess brought about a flood of images. The demon sucking away the last of my soul, Medjine charging across the park. She had a spear in her hands, ornate and ancient looking. She had driven it through the demon's ribs. Medjine had fought the demon off and saved my soul.

I peered down to see the Voodoo princess crouched at my midsection. She had my hand in hers, washing my fingers and sprinkling them with some sort of powder. The concoction caked onto my wet skin like concrete mix, then she wrapped it all in a loose linen. I was shocked to notice the cracks were gone. My hands looked whole, and except for the concrete poultice, they seemed to be back to normal. When she finished, she placed my bandaged hand on my chest and started wrapping the other one. I took a few deep breaths, trying to pull my thoughts together.

"What happened? I thought that thing—" I glanced back at Alex.

"Shhh...take it easy." Her hand rested on my cheek. "It would have if ..." her voice cracked, "if it weren't for Medjine. She saved you." A tear managed to escape her guard, and she wiped it away. But I saw that she held back more.

I shook my head, trying to remember the last few moments, then wished I hadn't. That sense of losing myself. Feeling that demon steal my soul while I was powerless to prevent it had been the worst thing I had ever experienced. Even worse than dying. When I had died, my soul had transferred, but I was still me. This felt different. It was like having my very essence stolen away. Everything that mattered. If I ever saw that demon again, I would pay it back in every kind of pain I could think of.

Medjine finished wrapping my other hand and laid it on my chest with the other. "Leave these bandages on for a couple of hours. That should give the powder plenty of time to work. You can take them off after that."

"The spear." I blurted the word out in amazement. "You threw a spear. How did you know where we were?"

Medjine looked at me. "These eyes see more than most, child. Most times it's a curse, but today they helped."

"Where did you get a weapon that would kill a demon? And do you have a dozen more?"

Medjine did not laugh. "My family passed that spear down for generations. It first belonged to my ancestral grandfather. He was a powerful Witch Doctor. He hid the spear away for a spirit who begged him to keep it safe. He and our family did so for centuries. Now the spear is back in the open, and there will be those who seek to possess it as their own."

"That demon," I said, realization dawning on me. "He took it."

It was a statement, not a question. Medjine had the answer written all over her face. "I'm sorry."

I didn't know what else to say.

"Not to worry, child. Things happen as they're supposed to. Perhaps the spear was meant to reveal itself in this moment. It may have a purpose we don't yet understand. It doesn't matter right now. Right now, you are the important thing. How do you feel?"

I smiled. "Actually, I feel pretty good. Great in fact. I'm a little hungry, and I wouldn't mind a bath, but other than that I feel good as new."

I sat up with Alex's help.

"No dizziness, pain, or unusual urges?"

I let out a chuckle. "I'm not sure what sort of urge you were expecting, but no. I think you drove that demon off just in time. I could feel everything—"

I glanced down at my bandaged hands unable to finish the sentence.

"One more second, and I wouldn't be here. Thank you, Medjine."

Alex put a hand on my shoulder.

"You were a lot closer than that. Medjine's spear didn't just injure the demon, it allowed your ... you to sort of leak out. The demon ran away, but you were all over the ground. Not blood but something else. Even I could see it. We only had seconds to act before you dissolved into nothing." Alex's voice caught in her throat, and tears welled into her eyes. She wrapped her arms around me and hugged me tight.

I put my arm around her and hugged back. "It's all right. I'm okay now."

I wasn't used to seeing Alex so upset. I must have looked horrible to her.

She let out a few sobs into my shoulder then pulled back and sat down next to me, wiping her tears away.

"We were so close to losing you. We didn't have any choice."

"What?" I smiled. "I don't understand. What did you have to make a choice about?"

Medjine offered me a soft smile and reached out with something in her hand. She had my locket clasped within her fingers. I wanted to reach out and grab it, but my hands were still wrapped up in King Tut's mittens. So Medjine looped the sturdy chain around my neck instead.

"We bound your soul to another, child. It was necessary to save you."

I glanced from Medjine to Alex. "Okay, how bad is it? Did you bind me to a stranger? Or—"

My eyes shot to Medjine again.

She laughed. "Don't look at me, child. I have enough curses hanging over my head without adding another. Besides, you don't want to be bound to a Witch Doctor. Spirits have a tendency to act a little different around us."

"Well, I know it wasn't you." I glanced over at Alex. "So, who is it?"

Just as the words came out of my mouth, a chocolate lab came bounding up and barged in between us to lick me in the face. He snuffed and huffed and wagged his tail, all while knocking Alex off balance with his wiggling butt.

"Whoa, boy." I reached up and pushed the affectionate dog away and couldn't help but laugh as I patted his head.

"You aren't so bad, are you? Are you going to be my new soul pal?"

I did my best to pet the dog despite my bulky dressings. He didn't seem to mind as he sat down, soaking up the attention.

"Oh, my gosh. I'm so sorry."

A voice came from behind me. I turned to see the bikini clad woman I had seen earlier now running up with a Frisbee in her hand.

"Chauncy, bad boy. You get over here."

Chauncy launched away as fast as he had arrived, hurrying over to meet his owner. She grabbed his collar as soon as he was within reach and waved at us.

"He's still a puppy. I'm trying to get him trained, but he just loves people."

Alex got up off her butt and crouched next to me again.

"That's okay. Have a good day."

She shot her a friendly wave, but as soon as they turned away, she lost her plastic smile.

"Wait," I said. "If it's not the dog then who?"

"Well, it's not the bikini girl, I can tell you that much."

I stared at Alex for a moment, and she let out a huff.

"We would have used her if she had been close enough. Either one of them, but they were too far away. We only had seconds. We had to use what was at hand."

I scanned the area and felt a tickle in my mind. Like a wiggle or a waddle, then a voice came out of nowhere and grumbled to life.

"I can't believe that blue-topped Skin Bag put her hands all over my feathers. It's going to take me a week to get that smell off."

I peered in the direction of the voice and witnessed the least majestic creature I had ever seen waddling up out of the lake. It looked just like the other mallards paddling mindlessly in the water, except this one was pitch black from bill to tail.

I wasn't sure if a duck could be fat, but this one waddled like it carried enough weight for three of its kind. The moment he laid eyes on me he stopped and stared, and I stared back at him.

"What's that guy's problem? I wonder if he has any bread?"

CHAPTER SEVENTEEN

"You have got to be kidding me." I stared at Alex, but she didn't say a word. I couldn't tell if she was trying not to laugh or cry.

"We had to use what we had at hand, child. Alexandrea is right. We had only seconds to save your soul. It was either this or lose you forever."

I looked back at the duck who seemed to be frozen in place.

"Hey." It flapped its feathers a little when it spoke into my head. *"Skin Bag. Can you hear me? Do ... you ... understand ... my ... words?"*

The duck drew out each syllable as if he were trying to communicate in some foreign land.

"This is not happening." I threw up my hands. "How do we fix this?"

As soon as I spoke, the duck screamed in my head.

"It can hear me. Somebody help. A Skin Bag broke the code. Take cover. Fly away. Fly away."

On the outside, the duck flapped its wings like a maniac and ran around in circles, quacking as if it had a fish stuck in its throat.

"You can't leave me saddled with this," I snapped. "You could have picked anything else. I can't believe this."

Medjine had taken to calling me child, but now I sounded like one. I couldn't help it. I was bound to a duck, and if her predictions were correct, I could never get away from it.

Medjine let out a huff as she packed her jars and vials into a cloth bag she had slung across her chest then stood up.

"Some thanks for saving your life, child. Enjoy your new friend. If I were you, I would take care of him. So far as I know, he is your only chance of remaining whole."

Medjine turned and stormed off. I went to stand and go after her. That's when I discovered I was not as recovered as I had thought. I managed to rise to my feet for about half a second before my legs crossed up. I spun around, and I was down again.

Alex leapt to my side in an instant.

"Medjine, please come back," I shouted. "I don't know what to do. Don't leave me like this!"

The Voodoo princess did not turn back. All I could do was watch her go. As soon as she stomped out of sight, I turned my glare on Alex.

"Before your mouth blabbers out something stupid enough to make me leave you sitting here all alone with your new friend, stop and consider the fact that we just saved you from a fate worse than death. It is not a perfect situation but stop whining and make the best of it."

I sat there for a moment and breathed. She was right. They had done what they could with what they had. Would I complain if I were missing an arm or a leg if someone saved my life? Probably, but I would turn another leaf. Afterall, how many people can say they can talk to a duck?

"I'm sorry," I said finally. "And thank you ... for saving me with this—"

I glanced over at the fat, feathered atrocity standing in the grass several yards away.

"It's a duck." She laughed. "You can say it. Duck isn't a bad word."

"Well, it's pretty close, and it makes me want to say bad words."

"Hey, Meat Shirt. We've already established that I can hear you."

The duck's voice in my head sounded low and gravely. Sort of like Danny DeVito if he had smoked way too many cigarettes.

"Right, sorry," I said, turning my attention to the duck. "Can you just hear me talking or can you sense what I'm thinking too?"

"I don't know. Have you thought anything comprehensible in the last twenty minutes?"

I gritted my teeth and thought about wrapping the word comprehensible around the duck's neck and squeezing. When it didn't react, I thought, "If we're going to get along maybe you should stop calling me things like Meat Shirt."

"But Meat Shirt is such a good name. What about Sun Bacon or Land Anchor?"

"Wait a minute." Alex chimed in looking between the two of us. "Are you talking to that thing? Is it speaking to you?"

"She's pretty. I don't usually like Land Walkers, but she has great plumage." The duck poked its beak toward Alex's Ty-D-Bol blue hair.

"Yes, I can hear it. He says you have great plumage."

Alex smiled at the duck. "Oh. Thanks. Does it have a name?"

I peered down at the duck awaiting an answer.

"If you're expecting me to understand her, you are going to be waiting a long time. I am a duck. I don't speak English."

"Then how can you understand me?"

"How am I supposed to know? One second, I'm doing a mating dance for some sweet looking mallards, and the next, that blue-head is nabbing me out of the water. If I weren't so muscular, I could have flown away."

"Muscular?" I scoffed. "Muscles don't droop. You're fat."

"I am not fat, and the ladies like a little insulation on their man. It keeps them warm at night."

"Can we just get back to a name? I'm Gabe, and this is Alex."

Alex raised up a hand and waved.

"I'm a duck. We quack. If we had names, they would all be quack. What sense would that make? Every time one of us sneezed, everyone would come running."

I groaned and put my head in my hands.

"What did he say?"

"He said his name is Quack."

"That is not what I said." Quack punctuated the statement with a wing flap and a quack of his own.

"See."

"Seems like a weird name for a duck," Alex said. "Don't they all quack?"

I let out a helpless chuckle. "Yes, they certainly do."

"I don't mean to break up this meet and greet, but if you're feeling well enough to stand, we might want to get out of this park. People are starting to stare."

I glanced around. "There is no one here."

Alex shrugged. "I know, but you're talking to a duck. It's just weird."

I rolled over and pushed myself up to my knees then got to my feet, careful this time not to let the world spin out from under me. It went much better this time, and I managed to remain in an upright, if not unsteady, position.

"I think we should all go back to the Voodoo shop and see what I can do about my new friend."

"What do you mean, all? I'm staying right here at the lake. You

can wander around those four-wheeled bird killers if you want to, but I don't go near the street. I stay right next to the water where cars can't float."

I peered down at Quack and fixed him with a sympathetic stare. "Like it or not, you and I are going to be joined at the hip for a while. I know you didn't ask for this, and even though you're just a duck, I feel bad that you are being held against your will. I don't like it much either, but if we work together, maybe we can find a way to fix this and get back to our normal—"

I was about to say lives but that didn't really fit for me.

"Let's leave it at, get back to normal. What do you say?"

Quack stared at me with a tilted head as if he were processing my words, then said, *"Just a duck? What is that supposed to mean?"*

"Let's go."

I turned and started to walk back out of the park the way we had come, and Alex followed along with me. Behind us, Quack kept pace, waddling on his little webbed feet and filling my mind with his chatter.

"What if I called you just a hair-topped skin-sicle? Would that be okay? I don't think so. Ducks have feelings. We have lives. Do you know how many kids I have? Granted, I don't take care of them, but that's what ducks do. I don't feel I should be judged for that."

I did my best to block out the ranting as we walked. With any luck, we would get to Medjine's shop quickly and find a way to return Quack to his estranged duck children before dark.

CHAPTER EIGHTEEN

I should have expected the Voodoo shop door to be closed when we got there. Why would Medjine storm off just to come back here and wait for us to show up? She wasn't the type to play games. If she wanted to make her exit, we wouldn't see her again until she was ready to be seen.

Truth be told, I owed her more than an apology. She had saved my soul. I owed her a debt almost too big to pay, and my debts were stacking up faster than I could count them. I did not look forward to the day when I had to pay them all off.

I went to knock on the heavy metal door, but my hands were still wrapped in the thick linens Medjine had applied at the park.

"Could you help me with these?" I turned to Alex and held my hands out to her. "She said I only had to keep them on for a couple of hours."

Alex raised an eyebrow at me. "Maybe we should keep them on a little longer. You could pretend you're a boxer."

"Ha ha." I kept my hands held out to her.

"Fine," she reached out and started unwinding the linens on my hand. "No sense of humor, I swear."

When she had them both free, we tossed the bandages into a nearby dumpster. The powder she had applied was dry again, so it only took a small effort to rub it all off my skin. When I finished, I examined my hands. Everything looked blissfully normal. No cracking, scabbing, or sores to be seen. There wasn't even any sign that a crazy demon had used my fingers as a teething ring. I shuddered at the thought. I was so thankful, I almost forgot about the other little side effect of my healing.

"Hey, could you two walk any faster?" The croaked voice panted out in my head. I so wished Alex could hear it, if for no other reason than to share my irritation.

"My legs are only about three inches long. Do you know how fast I have to move these things to keep up with you?"

I glanced back at Quack, who had just made his way into the alley.

"Why don't you use those feathery things you have instead of arms?"

Quack gasped. *"Oh, because I have wings you think I should use them? My wings are here for your convenience, is that it?"*

I rubbed my temples with the palms of my hands.

"What's wrong?" Alex leaned in and checked my eyes. "Are you feeling bad again? Do you need to sit down?"

"I'm fine," I grumbled. "Other than the feathered headache coming down the alley."

Alex turned to watch Quack waddle along the pavement and laughed.

"I don't know what you're complaining about. I think he's cute."

"Yeah. Well, he's not power-whining into your brain."

"I am not whining. I am stating facts. Like my legs are short, and you are a jerk."

I turned and pounded on the big steel door to Medjine's Voodoo shop out of sheer desperation.

"Maybe she's hiding inside, waiting to vaporize me with one of her potions."

I kept beating on the door with the side of my fist, rattling the rolling door so loud it echoed off the walls of the surrounding buildings. After a couple of seconds, Alex came up beside me and grabbed my arm.

"Keep that up, and someone will vaporize you with their fist."

I groaned and let my head rest against the door.

"It's not that bad." Alex patted my back in consolation, but I swore I heard the humor in her voice. "So, what if you have a new pet? Maybe you two will be best buds."

I raised an eyebrow and looked at her out of the corner of my eye without lifting my head off the steel.

"Best buds? It's a duck. When was the last time you hung out with waterfowl?"

"*Whoa.*" I felt something nuzzle in between my legs and glanced down to see Quack wedging himself between my feet. *"No need to be insulting. I didn't call you any names."*

"You have called me names I've never dreamed of ... Never mind, what are you doing?"

"I'm cold. Do you mind? What is that smell? Is that your feet? Don't Dirt Surfers ever take a bath? Water is not poison, you know. It wouldn't kill you to get wet once in a while."

Alex peered down at Quack as he made himself comfortable. This time the grin on her face was impossible to miss.

"How can you be mad at that?"

"Trust me. There is way more going on there than you think."

"Oh, look, you have a new friend."

This latest voice startled us all. Alex and I spun around to face the intruder while Quack flapped out of his comfortable position and screeched like a maniac.

Sammy held out her hands and took a couple steps back.

"Sorry about that. Bad habit. I'll try to wear a bell or something from now on."

"Where did you come from?" Alex looked around the alley as if searching for some doorway she could have popped out of.

Sammy pointed up the alley the same way we had come. "Up there. I saw that you two were here, and I thought I'd say hello."

I fixed a stare on Sammy, stepping in a little closer as I put my hands on my hips.

"I saw you in the park. You were there right before that demon hit me. Why didn't you do anything to help?"

Alex stared at me then at Sammy. I hadn't mentioned this to her yet, so she seemed a little taken off guard by the statement.

"I did help you, or at least I tried to. I warned you about the demon, did I not?"

"Yeah, just in time for the thing to hit me like a runaway truck. Why didn't you get Alex or fight it off yourself? Something tells me that giant flaming sword of yours would have made short work of something like that."

Quack walked up beside me and glanced up at Sammy.

"Who is this joker?"

I was about to tell him to clamp his beak shut when Sammy turned her eyes to meet that of the duck.

"I'm Sammy. I'm an angel. It's very nice to meet you."

My mouth fell open. "You can talk to it?"

Quack flapped his wings and backed up a step. *"I'm sorry. I didn't realize you were ... I didn't mean ..."*

"Don't worry. We're all friends here," Sammy said. "Have you taken a name yet?"

"He said his name is Quack." I piped in before he could answer.

"That is not what I said," Quack grumbled. *"And no, I have not agreed to a name yet."*

Sammy nodded. "Then I will call you Quack until you have chosen a name that suits you."

"I'm not sure if there is a name that suits a duck better than Quack but okay." I shrugged.

"Am I the only one who can't talk to your little friend?" Alex crossed her arms and looked almost pouty at the prospect.

"Trust me, you aren't missing anything."

Sammy nodded. "We do not make it a rule to converse with the wild beasts of the world, but angels do have the ability to speak to all of God's creatures. Sometimes it's necessary in order to convey an important message."

Sammy held up a finger and walked over to a patch of dirt that had blown into the corner. There was just enough for her to pinch a small amount in each of her fingers. When she stood again, she chanted something under her breath. She held her arms out in front of her and reached for Alex.

Alex, in turn, dodged her advance, but Sammy raised her eyebrows as if to tell her to stay still. She never stopped chanting.

Sammy reached out again, and this time Alex held her ground in a strained almost awkward stance. Sammy rubbed the dirt onto both of her ears and then retreated, finishing her incantation.

Nothing happened. No flash of light, no poof of smoke, no lightning crashed down from the clouds above. Just Alex, standing there with dirty ears.

"What was that supposed to do?" I peered over at Alex looking at the dark smudge on her earlobe. "If that was some kind of angel greeting, it was weird."

Sammy quirked a smile and looked at Alex. "Consider that a gift."

"Sorry, but I'm as confused as Gabe, which frightens me all by itself. What was that supposed to ..."

"Fun fact. Ducks can't hold their poop. In about five seconds, it's

going to get awkward, so I am going to excuse myself and head to the corner over there."

Quack turned and speed-waddled away while we watched him go.

"And don't stare, or next time I'll do it on your shoe."

We all snapped our eyes back up, and I saw a mix of wonder and disgust in Alex's face.

"Did you hear that?" I asked.

Alex nodded. "I am not sure I wanted to, but yeah."

"Like I said, you weren't missing anything."

I couldn't help but smile. At least I had a partner in misery. For that I was thankful.

"That was a nice thing to do, Sammy. Alex might not appreciate it after she hears some of the chatter that little guy produces, but thank you."

Alex nodded. "It's an incredible gift. Thank you."

Sammy nodded in response. "I hope it helps. You will be together for a very long time."

I tried not to look back over at Quack doing his business in the corner and tilted my head at Sammy. "How do you know what happened? I don't mean to be rude, but how long were you watching us in the park? And, once again, why didn't you lift a finger to help?"

Sammy offered us a sympathetic smile, turning her gaze from Alex and then back to me again.

"I'm afraid my place on this Earth is as an observer. I am not permitted to interfere with events as they unfold, especially if they are connected to your realm. Only a direct order from on high allows me to get involved."

"But you tried to warn me about the demon before it hit."

Sammy shrugged. "Sometimes I can't help myself. It wouldn't be the first time I was punished for interfering in Earthly affairs. Even the gift I just gave you could be seen as invasive. I'm sorry I couldn't help you, Gabriel. It was torture for me to watch, and I could not have been happier when your Witch Doctor came to the rescue. I thought you were lost, but she arrived in the nick of time and managed a perfect shot as well. One might say it was almost a miracle."

The way she said that last part sounded almost cynical or perhaps she knew more than she said. Either way, it was a tough spot to be in.

"So, if it is not too intrusive, mind if I ask if there's a way to reverse this binding without cracking my soul shell wide open again?"

Sammy shrugged. "I am no expert on Woebegone physiology, nor do I understand many things about the power of the occult. I can say that you seem to be cured of an affliction that would have destroyed you by the end of the day. That is a powerful gift in itself. Perhaps you should not take it for granted."

I blanched at the realization that I had been so close to losing myself even without the demon's help. Maybe Sammy was right. Maybe I should appreciate Quack as a gift and ally. I'm sure we could learn to be friends.

He waddled back toward us and ruffled his feathers. *"Sorry about that. Been eating too much bread lately. Wreaks havoc on the digestive system, but I can't resist the stuff. They are like little squares of heaven."* Quack turned an eye to Sammy. *"No offense."*

Sammy held up a hand. "None taken."

I made a note to keep bread out of Quack's diet from now on.

"I have one more question, if you don't mind." Alex looked from Quack to Sammy, avoiding any more conversation about digestive tracts.

"The world is a big place. How is it you always know when and where we're going to turn up? I understand the chance meeting the first time, but I am not buying an accident in the park and now here."

Sammy winced, looking more than a little guilty.

"I hope you can forgive me. I don't have an opportunity to talk to beings who understand the true scope of reality very often. So when I do, I like to keep track of them, so I can pop in and see how they're doing. It gives me someone to talk to, and I can sometimes help them along their way if it isn't too obvious."

"So, what are you saying?" Alex narrowed her eyes at Sammy. "You have some sort of tracker planted on us?"

Sammy let out a laugh. "No, of course not."

I found myself letting out a sigh of relief. I didn't have anything to hide ... at least, not here, but I didn't like the idea of anyone tracking my every movement either.

"I don't need a gadget to track you. You are the trackers. I can sense your body signatures where and when you pop into the Earthly realm. Sort of like spotting a face in a crowd, only the two of you are wearing bright orange and have a spotlight shining on you."

Alex stepped back shaking her head.

"Turn it off. Shut it down. Whatever it is you do. We aren't dogs on a leash. You want to talk to us, find another way. Call us on a telephone, send an email. Tracking our every movement is more than a hello. It's an invasion of privacy."

Sammy never lost that understanding grin as she listened to Alex make her plea. She stood and nodded listening to every word, but I could see that it would do no good.

"I can see that you are upset."

"Upset?" Alex began to ramp up from irritated to hostile, and I moved in close to her in case I had to save her from herself.

"Yeah, I'm upset. I just found out Big Sister is tracking us for her own amusement, like we were put here to entertain her. Upset is a word you might use to describe how I'm feeling. There is also angry, betrayed, aggressive, hostile ..."

I put a hand on Alex's shoulder as she started to take another step.

"Perhaps I should go. You have a lot to discuss. I am sorry to have upset you. Enjoy your gift. I will see you again soon."

With that, Sammy backed away a few steps then turned away to leave. She walked up the alley a few feet then exploded into a flock of grey pigeons. It was both a beautiful and awe-inspiring sight. At the same time, I had to wonder, why pigeons?

Alex did not share my admiration.

"I'm sure you will see us again!" She yelled down the empty alley. "You are tracking us like dogs. Stay away from us, you hear me. Take your impartial disposition and stay out of our way!"

CHAPTER NINETEEN

The second we stepped off the Envisage Splice Transport Elevator, Alex and I ran to the side of the wide hallway where no one could see us and yanked open the spacious black backpack we had procured Topside for our trip back to The Nine. We had no idea what would happen to Quack when we brought him down but leaving him Topside was not an option. Medjine had told us that we could not bear to be apart. I wasn't sure what that meant, but I didn't want to test the theory so soon after being healed. Alex and I figured it was best to keep Quack with us, but that meant breaking a big Agency rule. Maybe one of the biggest. Thou shall not usher a living being into The Nine.

The two of us peered down into the backpack together. I couldn't believe how worried I was about this duck's safety. Maybe I did have some sort of attachment to this feathered fiasco.

At first, it was almost impossible to see Quack's dark form among the shadows and black fabric of the backpack, but then he turned his head upward to peer at us with his shiny, little eyes.

"I don't know what you two were doing out there, but I have flown through a hurricane with less turbulence. You better find me a barf bag, or it's going to get messy in here."

I couldn't help but smile. "Take a few deep breaths. The nausea will pass. Believe me, I know how you feel."

Quack swayed his head back and forth on his long black neck. *"Ducks can't really throw up, but if I could, I would hurl all over your shoes."*

Alex leaned away from the top of the backpack, apparently unwilling to chance Quack's anatomical assessment on a duck's digestive capabilities.

"Why don't you get him out of here for a while? You don't want any of the Agents spotting your friend in there." Alex jerked a thumb over her shoulder. "Head over to Hula Harry's, and I'll meet you there."

"Hula Harry's?" Quack shifted inside his pack. We made enough room for him to sit on the bottom without having to contort himself into an awkward position, but just barely. *"Is that a beach hangout? I could use a good swim."*

I flopped the top of the backpack over and zipped it halfway to be sure Quack could still breathe.

"Sorry, but swimming isn't high on the recreation list down here. I'll do my best to fill you in on what this place is all about on our way to Harry's."

Alex raised an eyebrow at me. "That should be a fun conversation."

"You're the one who wanted to hear him. Should I wait until you're around again?"

Alex held up a hand. "No, no. That's all right. I've heard enough for now."

Quack hadn't stopped complaining from the second we had left the Voodoo shop. In fact, this had been the first break we'd had in the last couple of hours. Maybe there was an advantage to his nausea after all.

"*Hey. What are you two doing out there? If we're going, let's get a move on. Chop, chop. It's so hot in here my feathers are sweating.*"

Too bad it hadn't lasted longer.

"I'll meet you at Harry's." Alex had already backpedaled down the wide hallway. "We still have a job to do. I'll check up on a few things, and we can figure out our next steps from there."

She lifted her hand and pointed to the backpack. "Have fun with your conversation. Remember, honesty is the best policy ... until it's not."

"Thanks for the advice."

She smiled and turned away, disappearing around the corner, leaving me all alone with my feathered friend.

"Well, I guess we should head out too."

"*Try not to jostle me around too much. You walk like a flatfooted ogre. Put a little cushion in your step. It'll do wonders for your knees.*"

I swung the backpack around to my back with a little more speed than necessary. "I'll keep that in mind, thanks."

"*Whoa, just because I can't hurl out a lunch ball doesn't mean I can't do other things. Remember what I said about ducks holding their poop.*"

I sighed. "I may have to clean it up, but you have to ride in it till I do."

"*You have to let me out sometime, and I will never go back in. I can fly, remember? You might as well paint a giant, red target on the top of your head for me to aim at.*"

I grumbled as I made my way toward the door. "Let's just get going, and you tell me if you need to make any pit stops."

"*Will do. You're the boss.*"

The ride to Hula Harry's was long and full of strained conversation. I did my best to explain what had happened to Quack and why, who I was, and where we were. Ducks didn't have much of a philosophical belief concerning religion, Heaven, or Hell, so they were just places to him. One thing he could understand was the difference between dead and alive. To Quack, dead was dead, so the fact that I was up and walking around got a little confusing.

"So, you're telling me you're not alive?"

I swung Quack's backpack off my shoulders, more gently this time, and set it on a stool next to me at the bar. Dan saw me walk in, so he had already pulled out a glass and filled it with Dr. Pepper.

"Thanks, Dan." I nodded to my friend as he eyed the black backpack, I had brought in with me.

"Do I want to know what's in there?"

"Probably not."

"Hey, are we here? Let me out. It's so hot in here my ears are melting."

"I can't," I whispered. "You can't be out in the open. And do ducks even have ears?"

"Don't be stupid. Of course we have ears. Just because they aren't oversized skin wrinkles on the side of our head doesn't mean we don't have them. And why can't you let me out? No one in your town has ever seen a duck before? Unzip this bag, or there's going to be a big, green pool of you-don't-want-to-know in here."

I let my head fall back and sighed.

"You doing okay, Gabe?" Dan fixed me with a look of genuine concern. "Who are you talking to?"

I let out another groan and reached for the backpack. I unzipped the top and then lifted Quack out. He flapped his wings, stretched his neck, and quacked several times as I set him on the bar.

"Thanks for trying to stay incognito." I glared at him. "I'm not sure if everyone outside heard you. Can you try to draw a little more attention?"

"You try riding inside of a canvas envelope for a couple of hours. You're lucky I don't fly around the room."

Dan backed away until his body was pressed against the shelves of liquor bottles on the wall behind him.

"Is that a ..."

"Yes, it's a duck."

"But it's ..."

"Alive. For now, yes, he is."

"How ... but you can't ... why a duck?"

Quack turned his little black eyes on me. *"He seems agitated. Should I bite him?"*

"Do not bite him. Don't bite anyone."

I glanced around the bar and saw that just about every Woebegone in the place had stopped to stare as well. I felt like I was in an old west saloon when the piano quit playing and everyone stopped to stare at the guy who was about to get shot.

"This is Judas Agency business. Go back to your drinks and keep what you see here to yourself. Everything will be fine."

No one moved.

"Relax or leave, the choice is yours."

With that, the room erupted back into rumbled conversation, although half of them kept their eyes on the shadow black waterfowl. The only thing missing was the player piano.

I turned back to Dan and saw that he had not moved from his position against the wall.

"Not you too. You act like you have never seen a duck before. Take it easy."

Dan relaxed a little and took a step forward.

"Do you know what'll happen if someone catches you with that thing down here?"

"Not really, do you?"

"No, but I am sure it would be bad."

"Yeah, well, that's pretty much how I operate at The Judas Agency nowadays. This is Quack. He might be around for a while."

"Ask him if he has any mealworms or sardines back there."

Quack took a couple of steps toward the edge of the bar. *"I'm starving."*

"I thought you had to go use the little duck's room."

"Naw, I just wanted you to let me out. This is a cool place. Where's the beach?"

"There is no beach. I told you, we aren't really a fan of water in The Nine."

Dan held up a finger pointing between the two of us. "Wait a minute. Are you talking to—"

"Yes. I can talk to him. He can talk to me. We are conjoined soul-twins and get to be besties wherever we go."

A slow grin crept over Dan's face, then he let out a snort of laughter.

"What in the world have you gotten yourself into? Just when I think your Judas Agent stories can't get any crazier."

He let out another laugh.

"Ha, ha, I am glad you think this is so funny."

"I can't help it. I never pegged you as a bird guy."

He cackled out even more laughter.

Quack looked at me again. *"I don't understand what he is saying, but I still feel like I should bite him."*

"Give me a second, I'm considering it."

Before Dan could calm down, the door to the bar opened again. Alex walked in and sidled up beside me.

"I tried to catch you before you left. Plan B came through on our assignment. We need to leave right now to make our window in time."

"What do you mean Plan B? I didn't know we were done with Plan A."

Alex glared as she sat on the stool next to me.

"Weren't you listening when I told you about the graffiti and gang leaders? They didn't even ... Wait a minute, why is Quack out of his bag?"

Her expression changed from annoyed to panic so fast I thought she might leap across the bar to grab him herself.

"Quack is out of the bag because Quack likes to breathe." The little, black duck wagged his head back and forth as if to punctuate his point. *"And Quack is not my name, it's what I do. Is your name burp or fart? I don't think so."*

Alex turned to me then looked at everyone else in the bar who were still trying to act as if there wasn't a live being standing in the middle of The Nine.

"Have you lost your mind?" Alex smiled and leaned in close to me, showing her teeth in a way that meant anything but cheer. "I sent you away from The Agency so no one would see him, not so you could walk him around like the family pet."

"Yo. Watch it with the P word, lady. I am nobody's property. I am a free bird."

Alex looked over at Quack then leaned back and rubbed the bridge of her nose with her fingers.

"And you wanted to be able to hear him." I grinned.

"This still doesn't change anything. You can't have him out ..." She paused, caught herself and then turned her attention to Quack. "You can't be out in the open like this. The—inhabitants here are dangerous. They could hurt you. Even if no one here does anything, if word gets out that you're here, even more dangerous things will come looking for you. We have to keep you out of sight for your own safety."

Quack stared at me and somehow managed to look like he was putting his wings on his hips. *"Why didn't you tell me that in the first place? I could have hung out with your crazy friend on the other side of this counter where no one could see me, but you want to parade your new duck all over town."*

"What?" My mouth hung open, not knowing how to respond. "I never wanted to let you—this isn't my fault." I turned to Alex. "He is the one who wanted to get out. I wasn't showing him off, I swear."

"Let's just get going." Alex picked up the backpack and held it out to Quack who managed an indignant nod then jumped inside.

"We don't have much time to get Topside if my new plan is going to work."

CHAPTER TWENTY

"I still don't understand why we're at a hospital." Alex and I crouched in the dark, outside a rear dock area of the L.A. County Medical Center. We had found a dumpster in the shadows that hid us from anyone moving in or out of the staff entrance, not that people would be walking in at this hour. Anyone in their right minds would be snug in their beds.

"I thought you said we were going to frame a gang member for a fake robbery."

"We are." Alex waved for me to follow her and scurried up the ramp leading to the door. "I just didn't explain *how* we were going to frame him."

When we got to the entrance, Alex pulled out her robot phone. She called it an Android, and to be honest, I had never seen it turn into any sort of robot. But it did have a nice bag of tricks where new electronic locks were concerned.

I waited while she tapped the screen and accessed some sort of program. I had left this world in the eighties. There was such a thing as a cellphone, but it came in a giant suitcase, and the handset was attached to one of those curly wires that got tangled no matter how you stored it. I had pretty much given up on modern tech. It all felt so impersonal anyway. If I wanted to bust through that door, a foot and a little muscle would be faster and more effective. So what if it was a bit noisy.

I scanned the area for security or loitering employees and eyed a van sitting outside the building. Alex had said we would need a vehicle. I'd bet that one would do nicely.

A sign hung just behind it on the wall of the building as well. I squinted, trying to make out the lettering in the dark. When it came into focus, my eyes went wide with panic.

The sign read, "Morgue. No Anonymous Night Deposits. Sign In At The Front Desk."

I heard a click, and Alex pulled the door open with a grin. I did not return her expression.

"What are we doing at the morgue?"

"Morgue? What's a morgue? I can't see anything in here." Quack's voice broke through my anxiety, and I heard the zipper on top of the backpack move. Then with a rustle of movement, Quack's head appeared over my shoulder. *"That's better. It smells weird in there. We aren't going inside, are we?"*

Quack and I both turned our gaze to Alex who still held the door.

She let out a long breath. "I knew if I told you we were coming to pick up a *dead* gang member, you would go all squeamish on me."

"Does she mean dead, like you and her, or dead, like the gas bags they fish out of my lake once or twice a year?"

I tilted my head to look at Quack. "The second one. Now be quiet while I strangle my partner for not telling me what we were going to do."

Alex put a finger to her lips and then peeked around a corner. When she saw the coast was clear, she hurried across the hall and in through a set of stainless-steel doors, giving us no real choice but to follow. The sign on the door said, "Cooler." Underneath the printed sign hung another handwritten one that said, "No Eating, Drinking, or Pilfering." The residents here had a sick sense of humor. I'm sure I would have fit in fine, were it not for all the dead bodies.

We walked through the heavy doors and let them close behind us. Inside was a room covered in stainless-steel ... everything. There were long stainless-steel counters topped with stainless-steel cupboards. There was a deep stainless-steel sink and several stainless-steel gurneys rolled up against the wall. The lighting in the room was harsh, and the temperature seemed to be about twenty degrees cooler than the hall outside. The main attraction was the wall full of oversized drawers that resembled something like giant filing cabinets; although, I doubted they held manilla folders.

Alex turned around to face me the second we were all in the frigid room.

"I didn't tell you because I knew you would freak out. On the other hand, I took your Boy Scout morals into consideration and figured waiting for a dead gang member would be way better than killing one ourselves."

"Last time I checked, there wasn't a merit badge for grave robbing. This is not better than killing someone." I paused and thought about that for a second. "Okay, it's marginally better than killing someone, but we are desecrating a body."

Alex rolled her eyes. "We aren't desecrating anyth—"

We heard the footsteps at the same time and scurried to either side of the door. I had no idea what we were going to do if a jolly night coroner came waltzing in, but I was pretty sure we wouldn't charm him into looking the other way while we rummaged through his corpse drawers.

The footsteps got louder then receded and continued down the hall. I let out the breath I had been holding and glared at Alex.

She glared back and continued the conversation in more of a whisper.

"We aren't desecrating anything. This guy is a John Doe I picked up on The Judas System. He's actually a gang member who overdosed in a park, but he hasn't been identified yet. We're going to relocate him for a few hours, that's all. No chainsaws or party dresses. We just have to figure out where he is, preferably before someone comes walking in here to catch us. Unless you want to add coroner assault to your merit badge list."

Without warning, Alex pulled open one of the oversized file cabinet drawers set into the wall and out rolled a naked horror of wrinkled flesh and open eyeballs. The odor of decay was so thick it felt like a tidal wave heavy enough to knock me off my feet. My eyes began to water, and I tried to breathe through my mouth. But I could still taste the horrid aroma.

"Whoa. How about a little warning?" I turned around, but as soon as I did, Quack tried to scramble out of my backpack and over my head. I had no idea a duck could scream, but Quack managed a shriek that sounded like tires stopping on wet pavement.

"Don't shove me toward that thing. You look bad enough with all your clothes on."

Alex rolled her eyes and closed the drawer. "You're both a couple of babies."

"Whatever." I peeked over my shoulder, then turned back around when I saw that the body was gone. The smell lingered like greasy teenagers outside a liquor store though. "You can't just suck a dead guy out of the wall like that without warning someone. And how are you still breathing? Do you not smell the Rip Van Winkle B.O.?"

"If you two children can get it together, we are on a bit of a time crunch, remember?" Alex wore a devilish grin, but she couldn't quite hide her nasally voice. She breathed through her mouth as well. "I'm going to open the next one now. Are you ready?"

I squinted and leaned back while Quack hunkered down so low he barely peeked over my shoulder. "Ready."

Alex paused a second, then pulled the drawer open. This time the occupant was clothed in jeans, a white t-shirt, and a red jacket. He had a red bandana hanging out of his jeans pocket and several gold chains around his neck.

"This one's not so bad." Quack straightened a little and peeked down at the cadaver. *"He looks way better than the ones they pull out of the lake. He doesn't even have pond scum in his hair."*

"This is our guy. Go grab a gurney from that wall, and we'll roll him out of here."

"I still don't understand what we're doing with this poor guy. What does this have to do with a robbery? If you're planning to use him as a getaway driver, we might be better off using Quack."

"Don't you worry about that. Just drag him onto the gurney. Once we're in the van, I'll explain the rest of the plan. For now, let's get going before the night shift comes back around and catches us making a withdrawal."

"You're not funny," I said. Quack started making a noise that sounded like a cross between coughing and hiccups. After a second, I realized he was laughing.

"Great, not only do I have a duck as a new partner, but he has a terrible sense of humor."

"I don't know," Alex said. "He is starting to grow on me. Now get that gurney and let's go."

CHAPTER TWENTY-ONE

Alex and I stared down at our crime scene like an artist appraising his greatest masterpiece—if his masterpiece were set in the middle of a filthy shipping yard full of semi-trailers and Connex containers. Our van was parked with the rear doors open, to appear as if the heist had gone awry while our dead perpetrator lay in a jumbled mess on the concrete.

"Do you think we should stretch him out the other way?" Alex put a hand on her chin as she circled the scene. "Right now, it looks like he ran away from the truck, not to it."

"He looks like someone dropped him out of a hot air balloon. We are not creating a piece of performance art," I said. "It is a crime scene, and we're right in the middle of it. I'd like to remove myself from your little creative outlet as soon as possible."

Alex sighed and walked toward our John Doe. "Fine. Come over here and help me."

I followed her over, and together we pulled John into a sitting position.

"Okay, hold him right there."

Alex reached into her jacket and unholstered the LC9 Ruger she always carried to Topside missions.

I wasn't sure if I should drop John or hide behind him.

"What are you doing?" My words came out in a high-pitched shout.

"What? You think our guy keeled over from a heart attack? We have to make it look like the rival gang shot him or all of this doesn't work."

Alex raised her pistol at John, and I stretched as far away as I could, holding him up like a football for a placekicker. Turned out one finger wasn't enough to keep him steady. A shot rang out, but John had already ducked. The body had slipped out of my hand and fell back on the pavement with a sickening thunk, causing Alex to miss him altogether.

"Seriously? Alex eyed me. "Is something about this job confusing to you? Hold him still. I don't need a moving target."

"You try steadying him. It's like trying to hold a sack of squids."

"Just hold the dead guy still while I shoot him. Is that too much to ask? It's not like you're going to die if I hit you."

"That thing isn't loaded with fluffy balls of cotton." I reached down to try and adjust John into a target ready position again. "I might not die, but bullet wounds sting like getting kissed by a comet."

"I could shoot you now and end the suspense."

"It's murderey enough out here without you offering to shoot everyone. Can you just help me get him back up?"

"Fine." Alex let out an exaggerated sigh. "But I reserve the right to deliver that comet kiss if you drop him again."

Alex holstered her gun again and walked over to where I had gathered a handful of unwieldy arms and shoulders.

"I thought we weren't going to desecrate the body, anyway." Alex helped me wrestle John back up into a sitting position, but his head lulled over in an unnatural angle. "I'm sure I remember you saying something about that. What about this guy's family? I know he's a gang member, but I bet he has parents. I'll bet his mom never wanted him to get involved in this kind of life. Imagine how heartbroken she's going to be. Her little boy, gone at such a young age. He might even have a brother or sister. Someone who looked up to him. You want to put a bullet in his head just to sell your plan. Think of your own family. How would you feel if this was someone you loved?"

Alex stared at me, her hands wrapped into John's bright red coat as a handhold. After a second, she let go, and John thunked to the ground again.

"I hate you so much sometimes."

She got up without saying another word and walked toward a semi-trailer a few yards away. The lock on the rolling door appeared much too new. Considering everything around us was little more than rusted out husks, this thing looked thick enough to secure the Hope diamond.

"I just wanted to shed a little perspective on—"

Alex held up a single silencing finger and then took the lock in her other hand. She stared down at it, and after a few seconds, I saw the metal turn cherry red in her palm. Alex yanked it hard, and the whole thing fell apart in her grasp. I've said it once, and I'll say it again, her Topside power was so much cooler than mine. After coming so close to losing my soul, I wasn't sure I'd ever want to use my power again.

"I don't even know why I bring you on these missions. You just mix everything up with your morals, then pretty soon we're helping little, old ladies across the street instead of framing rival gangs for theft and murder."

"That seems like a stretch, but I'm sorry if I mess up your plans."

Alex threw the door to the trailer open and revealed row after row of stacked boxes labeled *Famine Relief*.

"I don't think you're sorry at all. I think you do it on purpose. I just wish my conscience would stop listening to yours."

I smiled as Alex climbed into the back of the truck.

"I don't mean to add insult to injury, but are you about to destroy a truck full of famine relief food?"

Alex scowled at me, then threw the first row of what were apparently empty boxes out of the trailer revealing very different kinds of crates behind them. These were heavy wood construction, long and flat, and marked with things like 9mm and AK-47.

"Whoa." I stood up, looking at the huge stash of weapons. "There has to be enough guns there to start a small war."

Alex grinned. "If all of this works out the way it's supposed to, they're going to need them."

"Hey, look who I found." Quack came waddling around the trailer like an overweight penguin.

I had let him out of the backpack to stretch his legs ... wings ... whatever he needed to stretch and find something to eat. Now he was back, and it looked like he wasn't alone.

Sammy rounded the corner of the trailer behind him, and the tension in the air got tight enough to lean against. "Wow, you two have upped your game. Now this is more like it."

"What do you want?" Alex jumped down out of the trailer and walked away from Sammy, not bothering to glance at her. "You here to critique our work or just stopping by to get a look at your favorite zoo animals?"

If Alex's venom stung, Sammy didn't show it. She just grinned and surveyed the scene, taking everything in.

"This appears quite believable. Nice work. I do have one question. How did your perpetrator die? Did he have a heart attack in the middle of the robbery?"

Alex shot a glare in my direction.

"He OD'ed," I said. "We figured he hit rock bottom at the wrong time."

Sammy nodded. "Actually, that could work. A single intruder has the misfortune of overdoing his chemical courage during the robbery. He may have even had a partner who abandoned him and the idea of the heist when his associate fell over dead. Bad luck like that can ruin a job."

"I'm glad you two are all warm and fuzzy over the plot twist, but an overdose does not put a rival gang on the hook for killing this guy. Which, if you remember," Alex gave me a hard stare, "was the whole point of this exercise."

"Hey, does anyone else hear that noise?" Quack interjected, but no one paid much attention.

"I don't think that'll be a concern."

"Oh?" Alex turned around to face Sammy. "And why is that?"

"Seriously." Quack walked over and stood on top of John Doe's chest. *"Is that thunder? Something feels wrong."*

"Because we are about to have a whole bunch of visitors. I came to warn you, but it seems I am a little too late."

Just as Sammy finished her sentence, I heard the rumble Quack had warned us about. It wasn't thunder, but something far more foreboding. It was the sound of dozens of motorcycles all converging on our position. We were caught red-handed ... again. Only this time the stakes were a lot higher than a little graffiti and a few cans of spray-paint.

CHAPTER TWENTY-TWO

Dozens of motorcycles rumbled into the shipping yard, circling like the Apache ready to strike. The noise was deafening as they revved their engines, kicking up sand and dust in a cloud of exhaust thick enough to make us choke. It would have been terrifying if we weren't already dead. I couldn't say as much for Quack or the angel. Of course, Quack could fly away, and I suspected Sammy had enough tricks up her sleeve to make this encounter less than worrisome as well.

After several rounds, one of the bikes broke off, swooped in, and stopped in front of us. The others followed suit one by one, forming a ring around us, the van, the trailer, and most importantly, our guest of honor, John Doe. As the bikes shut down, the rumbling storm of the Harleys subsided, leaving a palpable silence.

Alex, Sammy, and I all stood back to back creating a sort of human triangle while Quack held his ground atop John's chest. He probably figured he could escape skyward whenever he wanted to and had decided to stay and watch the show.

"Well, what do we have here?" The man on the first bike threw his kickstand down and slung his leg over the back of his

Harley to rise and face us. "Looks like we caught a couple of kiddies in the cookie jar."

The man wore dark sunglasses and a black bandana on his bald head. He had a thick black beard and leather vest which seemed to match every other biker in the crowd.

Blackbeard ignored our defensive position and peered down at John. He let out a whistle and then laughed.

"I think we've stumbled into a real conspiracy here, boys."

The men and women laughed all around us as they leaned against their handlebars, gas tanks, and sissy-bars, looking as relaxed and dangerous as a pride of hungry lions.

"What have you done to our poor friend here?" Blackbeard addressed me since I happened to be the one facing him at the moment. "Did you bore him to death?"

"We could ask you the same thing." Alex chimed in before I had a chance to answer. "We're a long way from your territory. If you're caught nosing around here, there's going to be a lot of trouble."

Alex was right. I hadn't even realized this wasn't the gang we were here to antagonize. This gun stash didn't belong to them, so why were they here? Unless they planned to heist the guns for themselves, and we happened to be in the wrong place at the wrong time.

"Oooooh." Blackbeard taunted. "Did you hear that? We're gonna be in big trouble if we get caught."

The crowd laughed again, and Blackbeard paced around to face Alex.

"I don't think it's us who should be worried right now."

"I think you're in rival territory with a dead gang member at your feet," I said, drawing his attention back to me again. "We might be in trouble right now, but the evidence is going to point to you in the long run. What sounds more believable? Three nobodies planted a corpse outside a gun dump, or the fact that you and your buddies set this whole thing up as a cover for stealing these guns?"

Blackbeard walked around to look at me again and nodded. "You have a point. How would we erase all these tracks? No doubt someone saw us ride into town. There's no way for us to claim we weren't here at the scene, especially once we show up with all of their guns."

"Right, so why don't you move on, and we'll ..."

"Unless." Blackbeard shouted out the word, interrupting me mid-sentence. "The owner of these guns sent us to get them."

As he finished his sentence, I heard the tell-tale growl of a semi-truck in the distance. A transport for the trailer we had just opened.

He grinned at me and patted me on the head like a little kid.

"Funny thing about the government. You're big, but that makes you a little slow. You can keep trying to spark gang wars, but here's the thing, we're all one now. We all work under the law of Marcella. We're way past infighting. We recognize what the government has done to us all these years. Holding us down, keeping us from flourishing by our own right. But it won't work anymore."

Blackbeard paced around us, basking in the stage set by his surrounding members.

"Marcella taught us to fight for our freedom the same way our ancestors did. The U.S. struggled under the oppression of the British all those years ago, but they broke free only to form an oppressive arm of their own. We will break free again. We will free ourselves from the heavy-handed government who seeks to divide us. We will band together and remind them what it means to be a real American."

Blackbeard stopped and stared into my eyes, looking like a drooling lunatic, but the circle of bikers erupted in cheers. He stood there like that until the accolades died down and then stepped forward, tilting his head to the side.

"What do you say to that?"

"I say you're all off your rockers and are in need of some heavy medication."

Laughter from around the circle and even Blackbeard himself.

"Sammy, I know you are not allowed to get involved with these sorts of things, but do you think you could make an exception this once?"

"I can't influence the outcome of an event like this. I'm sorry."

I felt my shoulders fall. On one hand, I knew there was almost nothing these men and women could do to harm us. We were all but impermeable to mortal weapons or any sort of damage as long as we were Topside. We would heal almost instantly if any harm came to us.

On the other hand, leaving a big pile of dead bikers in the middle of a shipping yard had a tendency to draw attention. We represented The Judas Agency; the largest terrorist organization the world had *never* heard of. Keeping it that way was part of the gig. If we left even a single witness after walking away unscathed, it would raise the sort of questions real governments would send people in black suits and sunglasses to investigate.

Turned out my line of thinking was in a whole different zip code from Alex's. She stepped out of our defensive position, held her hands high over her head, and manifested a huge ball of molten flame above each of her palms.

"Enough talk. If it's a fight you want, come and get it."

CHAPTER TWENTY-THREE

Revealing an unnatural command of the fiery elements usually elicited a certain amount of trepidation, even panic, but Blackbeard only took a step backward and stared at the flaming orbs as if he were seeing the world's best magic trick performed live in front of his eyes.

"Wow. That is impressive."

Alex let her hands drop to shoulder level, but she did not turn down the heat. If anything, she cranked it up a notch. "You want to see impressive? Watch how I turn you into an impression of a sixteenth century witch."

Blackbeard held out a finger and took another step back, betraying his unease.

"There is something you should know about us." Blackbeard paused to be sure Alex wouldn't toss one of her flaming basketballs and then went on when she held fast. "Marcella told us we might run into some ... shall we say ... extraordinary resistance. She never said it would be quite so spectacular, and she thought it might come later, but here you are."

That was enough to take us all down a notch. Who was this Marcella that she should know anything about a Judas Agent and our powers—or were they talking about Sammy? Perhaps they expected more heavenly intervention if death and destruction was on the menu.

"Marcella told us that all the guns, knives, and grenades in the world wouldn't hurt you."

I did not like where this was headed, and I broke formation to stand behind Alex. Sammy did the same, but we both kept our eyes peeled all around us, so none of the bikers could sneak anything in from behind.

"But we do know one thing you are vulnerable to." Blackbeard snapped his fingers, and one of the bikers walked up and handed him a small, handheld fire extinguisher. It wasn't one of the red, store bought jobs full of that messy powder, but rather an old-style water extinguisher. As he took it in his hands, I saw several other bikers pulling similar extinguishers out of saddle bags or makeshift holsters.

"Can you guess what this contains? I'll give you a hint. It isn't tap water."

Niners may not be vulnerable to normal injury, but there was one thing we could not abide: rainwater. Something about the way we were made up, or the way The Nine worked, that made rainwater like industrial strength acid to our skin. A few drops were enough to hurt us, an extinguisher full of the stuff, and we would melt like the Stay-Puft Marshmallow Man.

Blackbeard unclipped the nozzle and aimed it at Alex's face.

"Now, why don't you put out that road flare, and we'll make this quick for you?"

I had no idea how they knew our weakness, but I didn't have time to care. We had about a half a second before at least two of us went the way of hot candle wax. I didn't know what rainwater would do to Sammy, and Quack would probably thank them for the shower, but Alex and I would be dead ... again.

We all stood there staring at each other for a moment then I reached a calming hand toward Alex's shoulder. My intent was to find a diplomatic solution to this standoff, but when I touched her, I must have startled her instead. Alex's basketball sized fire orb bloomed into an atomic flame bubble the size of a dinosaur, flash burning everyone's retinas and threatening to singe off my eyebrows along with every hair I had on my head.

I screeched in surprise, and so did Alex. She jumped almost higher than I did and squelched the flames with panicked flaps of her arms. The disruptive effect was not to be lost on Sammy though. She exploded into a cloud of coos and flapping feathers as she dissipated into her pigeon form.

For a moment, I thought she had decided to save her own skin but then the flock of grey feathers and flying poop banked around to bombard Blackbeard's head, obstructing his view. He squeezed the handle on the extinguisher to further the chaos, but instead of blasting us with a face full of rainwater, he wound up spraying the stream into the air in an attempt to ward off the myriad of tiny claws scratching at his face and eyes.

So much for remaining impassive. We stood there for a second in shock, then Alex turned and sprinted in the opposite direction.

"Run!"

I followed suit as she reignited her fireballs and hurled them at the closest bikers about thirty feet away. They dove to the sides to escape the napalm bombs, laying their bikes down in the process. Another biker managed to keep his head and charged in to line up an extinguisher shot to our left.

That's when a black cannonball of a bird streaked by and hit the biker square in the face. Quack had turned midair at the last second, allowing him to smack into the biker with his webbed feet and voluminous duck-weight while squawking like an alarm clock gone horribly wrong.

I was about to make a break for the space Alex had cleared with her fireballs when I felt a hand grab my coat. Alex hauled me back and redirected me toward the open van doors in the middle of the biker melee. I jumped in one side, and Alex jumped in the other. With the doors closed, we were safe from any aquatic onslaught, but that would only last as long as it took for them to break the windows.

I glanced out at the symmetric circle still formed by their parked Harleys. There was barely enough room to walk between them. At the time, it had been an intimidating ... even impressive show of precision and force. Now they just looked like a big circle of Dominos.

"You thinking what I'm thinking?" Alex drew her gaze from the motorcycles outside as she started the engine.

I shook my head. "What a waste. Do it quick. Don't draw out the agony."

Alex revved the engine and dropped the transmission into gear as a few of the bikers reached the van. The tires let out a howl of smoke and rubber, then we smashed into the Harley parked closest to our front bumper. The impact jarred the van like we'd hit an old farm tractor, but the bike, as well as a half-dozen others, slid across the asphalt and carried the blow into the bikes parked next to them. Many of the bikes still had their riders attached, but they couldn't react in time to get out of the way. They were trapped in the mangled mass of toppling Harleys.

Alex swerved away among a hail of gunshots. Apparently, they weren't all that convinced about our imperviousness to lead after all. That, or they were just hoping to disable the van.

As soon as the jumbled mess of leather and steel faded out of sight, I reached out to grab Alex's arm.

"Okay, stop for a second."

"What's wrong?" She slammed on the brakes and looked at me as I rolled down the window.

Quack came swooping in and made a perfect landing on my lap.

"He was up above us. Don't ask me how I knew that."

Alex slammed on the gas again, grinning like a maniac. "You really came through for us back there, Quack. We owe you one."

"Owe me one? That guy came out of nowhere. I just wanted to escape. Who ever heard of people trying to kill each other with squirty cans? I used to think your kids were crazy, running around squirting each other with those plastic water shooters, but you people are the real lunatics. It's water!"

"I'll explain later." I gave Quack a light pat on the head. "For now, just know that you did good. Thank you."

"Whatever. Why don't you pay me back by getting me something to eat? I'm starving."

I looked over at Alex. "You know Quack isn't the only one we owe for that miraculous escape. And what was with that fire sneeze? You almost fried my lips off."

Alex snorted out a laugh. "I have no idea. I was out of ideas then you bumped into me and boom."

She smacked the steering wheel by way of illustration.

"Well, next time you feel a flame attack coming on, warn me. I'll step back a hundred yards or so."

I stared at her for a moment in silence waiting for her to acknowledge the fourth member of our escape crew.

After a second, she peeked at me out of the corner of her eye and groaned.

"Don't worry. I'll thank Sammy next time we see her. But that does not excuse the fact that she is still tracking us like a couple of endangered sea turtles. We need to address that issue in the near future. Either she agrees to stop stalking us, or we are going to have to stop it for her."

Much as I hated to admit it, she was right. We couldn't have an angel showing up every time we went Topside to carry out a Judas Agency mission.

"Agreed, but let's talk to her first. She seems reasonable. I'm sure she'll understand why we don't want to be tracked all the time."

Alex grumbled something unintelligible.

"What was that?"

"I said, fine. But for now, we need to figure out what's going on. If this Marcella knows who we are, then this whole thing might be a lot bigger than we think. We need to get back to The Agency and do some serious digging."

I nodded in agreement. In fact, there was one person who needed this information more than anyone else. Judas was in the know about a lot of things, but this one had slipped through his net. I needed to get back and brief him on the events unfolding up here. I knew all too well the consequences of letting things go. He needed to hear about Marcella and these gangs, and the sooner, the better. He might even have a few ideas on what we should do next. If we didn't get a handle on the situation, I had a feeling all these little surprises would start stacking up into one big boom.

CHAPTER TWENTY-FOUR

lex and I stood in The Judas Agency locker room. It was late; the kind of late that felt like no matter where we went, we weren't supposed to be there. Not a soul stirred anywhere. It was so spooky quiet that I even caught myself tiptoeing as I walked.

"We have to figure out who this Marcella is." Alex ran a hand through her hair and yawned. "She seems to be the key to this whole thing. I searched for her once and came up empty. I guess I need to dig a little deeper."

I nodded and returned her yawn with one of my own. "I say we turn in and hit it first thing in the morning."

I was exhausted, and I could see that Alex was too. Even Quack had settled down into the bottom of the backpack and fallen asleep.

"I hate to admit it, but I don't think I'd get much done tonight. What are you going to do with your little pal back there?"

I glanced over my shoulder at the backpack. "I guess I'll keep him with me and hope he's not a sleepwalker. I have no idea how much sleep a duck needs, but he already has a head start on me."

Alex chuckled. "Wait till he needs a bathroom break in the middle of the night."

I let my head fall back, and I stared at the ceiling in frustration. "He said ducks can't hold it. I don't know if he was serious, but either way, it is going to make for a fun night. Maybe I should find a newspaper for him to sleep on or something. I don't suppose you know if duck poop stinks?"

"If it smells like any other bird poop, don't plan on making new friends in the morning."

"Great."

Alex let out a little laugh again then put a hand on my shoulder. "Look, I'm sorry we couldn't find a better companion to join you with. If we had any other choice, we would've taken it."

I nodded. "It's all right. The little guy's sort of growing on me. He really saved our bacon tonight, whether he meant to or not. Just don't tell him I said that."

"I'm glad you're okay. That's the important thing. I know I don't say it enough, but I don't know what I'd do without you. You're more than a partner to me."

"Wow, you must be tired."

Alex backhanded me in the chest and smiled. "I'm serious."

"Sorry." I turned to face her and peered down into her eyes. "The feeling's mutual. Thank you for saving me."

We stood there like that staring into one another's eyes, no one around, in the silence of the night. I could hear her breathing, smell the lavender honey fragrance of her skin. Her lips parted, and all at once, I couldn't stop myself.

I reached out and pulled her in close to me, meeting her lips with mine. The feeling was so electric, it made me gasp. She took in a sharp breath as well, and for a second, I was sure she would reach up to meet my affection with a right hook. But then she leaned into me, and in that moment, we were one. Our bodies, our breathing, our heartbeats, all moving to fuel our passion for one another. It was the single most intense moment of my entire existence, and I never wanted it to end.

The kiss deepened, and when I went to take a breath, it was Alex who pulled me back down by my hair, unwilling to let me go. Finally, when the moment could not stretch any longer, we parted, both of us breathing heavy. My lips longed to rush back again. Suddenly, it seemed like torture not to kiss her, and I wondered if she felt the same. I was about to give in to the longing when something stirred at my back.

"What are we doing? Are we home yet? Why is it so hot in here?" Quack's timing was impeccable.

I let out an exasperated breath. Alex put a hand on my chest and gave me a gentle push backward. My arms, which had found their way around her body, slid away and fell back to my sides. I found myself wondering what Duck a l'Orange would taste like.

"You should get to bed and so should I." Alex cooed in a voice so smooth it was almost a whisper.

"I agree. We should go to bed." I winked, and she laughed.

"Go take care of your new friend. I'll see you bright and early in the morning."

Alex took a few steps backward.

I nodded and resisted the urge to chase her. "See you tomorrow."

She waved, and I watched her go, wishing I could pull her back into my arms and wondering what might have happened had I not had a duck stashed in my backpack.

"What was that all about?" Quack invaded my less than pure thoughts, and I was ever so thankful that words were the only thing my feathered friend could glean from my brain. *"If that was some sort of mating dance, it was terrible. You humans have no idea how to attract a mate. I have seen it firsthand. All that pink skin*

gyrating and wiggling with lots of loud noise. It's obscene. If you want to see a real mating dance, I can give you some pointers."

I turned and headed out toward my own apartment. "Thanks for the tip, but I think I can hold my own. What do you say you and I find you a nice newspaper to settle down on, and we can get some rest?"

"Suit yourself, but if we're going to stay together, we're going to have to talk about nesting arrangements. I'm not sleeping on a newspaper for the rest of my life."

I sighed. "Don't worry. I will find you a nice, cozy basket or something."

"And water. I'm a duck. I need to get wet. I don't see you avoiding the dirt."

"Okay, okay." I rubbed my temples. "I'll figure out the water thing too. Let's just stop talking."

"Fine."

I made my way up the hall to the apartments as thoughts of Alex filled my head. Sleeping with a duck was not the way I would have chosen for this night to end, but it could have ended a lot worse. At least I had something to dream about. That kiss was an unexpected surprise. I just hoped Quack didn't talk in his sleep.

CHAPTER TWENTY-FIVE

I woke up the next morning in my apartment/sleeping coffin with Quack still snug in his backpack. My brain seemed determined to keep me wide awake after only a few hours of shuteye ... or at least make it impossible for me to sleep. Wide awake implied I wasn't exhausted, and that was a gross misrepresentation of my current condition.

If sleep wasn't on the menu, doing something constructive might as well be. It was early, but I never took Judas for being a late riser. I bet he got into the office so early even the worms weren't awake yet. He would want to know about our latest development concerning this Marcella character. He wouldn't be happy about the unification of the gangs either. Judas had said my mission had better come off without a hitch, but there had been nothing but hitches since the mission started. At least it wasn't my fault for once. He may not like it, but he needed to hear about it. I just hoped he wouldn't take his frustration out on any of my tender parts while I was there.

I did my best to open the hexagonal shaped door at the end of my sleeping tube and slide out without making a sound.

There was no point in waking Quack. After yesterday, he had to be exhausted. I would hurry up to Judas's office, give my report, and get back before he knew I was gone.

The area outside the apartment was carpeted floor to ceiling in a deep shade of red. It not only kept the light dim, but the thick shag silenced any sound in the common area, making it easy for me to slip out. The second I closed the door, I felt an uneasy pang of anxiety. It started in the back of my neck, like the tingle of some foreboding event. Right now, it was just a spark, but I could tell the feeling would fan into a forest fire of panic if I didn't keep it under control—if I could control it at all.

I stood there for a moment and considered taking Quack with me. The fear of being away from him dug into my subconscious and tied thick knots in my stomach. I didn't want to acknowledge that Quack could be more of a weakness than a companion. I denied my baser instinct and walked away. This would not rule me. I'd do what I had to and then come back of my own volition. My existence would not be dictated by this bond.

I stomped off down the hall, ignoring the growing anxiety in my brain. Once I changed into my regular clothes in the locker room, I marched on toward Judas's office. I didn't get three steps before Alex rounded a corner and all but ran into me. My edgy nerves made me jump like a cat, then the sight of her brought about a whole new avalanche of emotions that had nothing to do with my nerves. Memories of the previous night's kiss stomped all over the forefront of my brain. One glance at the distressed expression on her face, however, told me our kiss was the last thing on her mind. Rather than make things weird, I decided to force my feelings back into the cold shower where they belonged, at least for now.

She wore the same clothes from last night, and her hair was mess. A far cry from her usual impeccable appearance.

"Gabe, you have to see this." She shoved her Android phone toward my face so hard I thought she might break my nose.

"Are you okay?" I dodged her phone jab then put my hand on her shoulder. "Have you even slept? You look terrible."

That stopped her for a moment, and she glared at me.

"I mean in a good way. Well, not good, but I mean I am concerned because you don't look good." I put my face in my palm. "Never mind. It's too early to put words together."

A few Agents began to dot the common hall filled with marble and more marble. Their footsteps and whispers echoed off the shiny walls almost as loud as ours did, and I hoped they were too preoccupied, or that it was just too early, for them to pay attention to our awkward conversation.

Alex pulled my arm off her shoulder and yanked me to the side of the hall, before shoving her phone in front of my face again.

"Never mind that. Look at what happened in L.A. after we left last night."

The screen on the phone came to life in colors more brilliant than I had ever seen. It was like watching a theater movie, only in the palm of her hand. I wanted to reach out and touch it. Test the screen to see if it were real.

I extended a finger to do just that, and Alex slapped it away.

"Will you stop geeking out and pay attention to the story?"

"Right, sorry." I refocused on the news report playing out on the small screen. Buildings were ablaze, cars were overturned, and I recognized the telltale linens that signified rows of covered bodies lying in the street.

"I don't understand." My mouth hung open as I stared at the carnage. "How did this happen?"

"Sorry, let me turn up the sound." Alex thumbed a switch on the side of the phone, and a reporter's voice came to life.

I tried not to be amazed at the clarity of that as well.

"*... an anti-MiRACL demonstration turned violent last night* *when armed protesters opened fire on police, leaving twenty-three dead and countless others wounded. Riots moved through the city unchecked for hours until the governor imposed martial law, allowing troops to move in and retake control of the streets."*

"Several areas remain closed this morning as crews struggle to contain fires and search for more wounded or dead. We expect civilian casualty numbers to rise throughout the day. We go now live to the City Mayor for ..."

Alex thumbed the volume down and pointed to the screen with her other hand. "I have been combing footage of these riots all night. They were peaceful until a band of armed lunatics came in and started shooting. They didn't even bother to disguise themselves. They were all gang members but not just one gang. I saw all different colors and some of the bikers we ran into last night. They all worked together."

I shook my head. "Unbelievable. What did the protesters do when all the shooting started?"

"That's the crazy part. At first the crowd seemed disoriented and scared, but then they fell right in and joined the violence. Gabe, they lit apartment buildings and houses on fire. That mob was out to kill as many people as they could, and I'm not just talking about the guys with the guns. Those are regular people with normal lives who were somehow inspired to commit mass murder."

I stared at her not knowing what to say.

"What are we going to do about this?" Alex let her hands fall to her sides and got right up in my face when I didn't answer. "This Marcella is doing more than joining a few gangs together. Somehow, she is motivating innocent people to go out and kill."

My eyebrows rose so high they felt like they were on top of my head. I took a step back and put a little space between us again. Alex still clutched her phone like she wanted to crush it with her bare hand.

"Forgive me for tripping up a bit here, but aren't you the one who usually suggests we do nothing in a situation like this? Not that I'm complaining, but why the sudden change of heart?"

Alex's took on the expression of a wounded puppy, and I was sorry for every word I had said.

"So, sue me if I have grown a conscience. You and I almost derailed a train into a town because I thought it would help my career here at The Agency. When we stopped it, I decided then and there that I did not want to be that person anymore. People are dying up there, and we are the only ones who know why. If you don't want to help me, then I am happy to figure it out on my own."

I moved closer to her and put my hands on her arms to calm her down. Her voice was rising to amphitheater levels in the echoed space of the hall, and as much as I wanted to see the violence stopped, we couldn't go full on anti-activist. Judas had warned me against any convenient resolutions to this mission. If Alex and I rode in with our hero badges blazing, The Council of Seven could turn an eye on The Agency, and that I could not allow.

"Take it easy. I'm with you. We just need to step back and make sure we're doing the right thing. Don't forget, our assignment was to instigate the gangs into killing each other. Maybe Sammy has the right idea. Why are we going to interfere in something that has nothing to do with us? This unification deal was in play way before we got there. Should we really be up there straightening out their mess?"

"That was different, and you know it." Alex shook her head and started to back away from me. "There are innocents involved now. If you want to sit here and relax while they die, that's fine. Why should we get involved? Because it's the right thing to do. I thought you of all people would understand that."

Alex turned and walked away before I could say another

word. I thought about chasing her, but it wouldn't do any good. What could I say? She was right. We should go help. It was the right thing to do. I wanted more than anything to stand beside her and fight. Thanks to Judas and his concern about The Council, I wasn't in a position to do it.

CHAPTER TWENTY-SIX

When the elevator opened onto the top floor of The Judas Agency tower, I almost reached out to push the button to go back down. Not because the thought of meeting Judas had become overwhelming. It was Quack. Every nerve, cell, and hair follicle screamed that being away from him was wrong. It felt like something bad would happen ... was happening ... and by being separated, I was to blame for the horrific result. Logic told me these things had to be untrue ... probably. Quack was locked inside my apartment, safe and sound, but that didn't matter. Being away from him felt like bending my elbow inside out, and I had no idea why. Anything that unnatural was wrong in ways even I didn't understand.

I stood inside the elevator for a full minute trying to decide what to do before the decision was made for me.

"Mr. Gantry." Judas Iscariot's personal assistant sat at the far side of the macabre waiting area fiddling with paperwork. She did not glance up at me but knew it was me, nonetheless.

"If you're thinking of retreating back to the lobby, that elevator works on a timer. Once it arrives, it stays for a predetermined period. We find it best as many of Mr. Iscariot's visitors tend to change their minds once they arrive."

I was tempted to push one of the buttons anyway, just to test the theory. But I figured, what was the point? I needed to get this meeting over with, and the sooner I got in there, the sooner I could get back to my duck.

Even thinking something that ridiculous made me want to throw up a little.

I wiped the sweat off my forehead and started into the room. Judas's assistant motioned toward the ornate office door across from her.

"Mr. Iscariot is waiting for you. He's a bit on edge today, so I would be careful if I were you."

I looked at her and remembered her strange ability to know pretty much everything that happened everywhere. I wondered if she knew about Quack, or the condition he had subsequently cured. If she did, how much, if any, of that information had she passed onto Judas?

The questions burned in my brain, but I couldn't ask them without revealing my secret, if they were even secrets at all. The whole thing gave me a headache. I decided I would just find out the hard way and altered my course for Judas's door.

I didn't bother trying to knock. The door always opened when I got there. I really needed to figure out how he managed that trick.

"Mr. Gantry." Judas's voice erupted from around the corner. "So good of you to join us. Sit down."

I hurried into the office and saw Judas flanked as usual by his two Hellion counterparts behind his desk. Procel never gave me a second glance, but Mastema's welcoming homicidal grin sent a chill up my spine. I wasn't sure if it was my imagination or not, but I swore her smile had grown a little broader since we had had our chat outside Hula Harry's.

"Please." Judas stood from his own high-backed office chair

and motioned to the bone chair opposite his huge ebony desk. "Sit down."

It was not a courteous offer but rather a demand shrouded in manners. If I defied the order, it would only light the powder keg waiting to explode beneath that impeccable black on black silk suit.

Judas walked around to the front of his desk as I sat down. I always hated it when he did that. At least when he sat behind his desk, there was about a mile of obsidian tabletop between us. When he stood right in front of me, the only thing between his hand and my throat was air.

"I have received several disturbing reports concerning the area you have been assigned to."

I nodded and rubbed my arms as though I were cold, but in truth my mind was on Quack. I wondered if this was what a heroin addict felt like when they went too long without a hit. My whole body itched like it crawled with bugs, only on the inside of my skin not the outside. I had to make a concerted effort to still my hands and keep from rocking back and forth in anxious frustration.

"Things have gotten a little hairy Topside. Our original plan to trigger infighting among rival gangs is pretty much out the window."

I watched Judas clench his right fist so hard I swore it creaked like old leather. Considering his warning about following through on my job, I figured I better explain faster if I didn't want the air barrier between us to disappear as well.

"It had nothing to do with our actions. There's another player in the game up there. Someone named Marcella. No matter how hard we try, we can't dig anything up on her. It looks like she managed to unite the gangs somehow and is trying to turn them into some sort of anti-government movement."

That drew a long pause where I was tempted to barricade

my neck with my hands ... just in case. My feet wanted to run right out the door as well, but I was determined to finish this meeting. My duck addiction had to wait.

"I would say after last night, this Marcella is not so much trying as succeeding. Street gangs and protesters have destroyed half of Los Angeles, killed police, and murdered bystanders. That's hardly the work of a few rabble rousers."

I resisted the urge to comment on his vernacular, even though the term rabble rousers had been a dork magnet even when it was in vogue. See, I could get better.

"We discovered the same thing this morning. We were up in L.A. last night and ran into part of their new-age gang army, but we had no idea they planned to launch an attack on the city."

I paused for a moment, wondering if I should tell him the part about the gang knowing we were from The Nine. Considering how things had gone in the past when I withheld information, I figured full disclosure might be the best policy.

"There is more."

Judas raised an eyebrow but left the comment open. I took that as an invitation to continue.

"The gang we ran into last night knew who we were, or at least where we were from. They knew our weakness and were ready to exploit it. We barely escaped in one piece."

Judas's expression pinched into a scowl as he considered this new bit of information.

"I hope you don't mind me saying this, but I wonder if The Council is involved with this whole operation. Who else would know about our weakness to rainwater and want to cause this level of destruction?"

Judas shook his head. I half expected him to blame me for this entire fiasco, but I was relieved to see he seemed as focused on finding the real culprit as I was.

"The Council of Seven makes no sense. Those protesters stood against MiRACL's inoculation program. We already know

The Council is backing MiRACL. Why would they build and support a militant organization bent on rising up against them?"

I shrugged and scratched my arm again. "Who then? I can't think of anyone with the clout or power to organize against us."

"There must be someone we have all overlooked. We need to figure out who it is before they manage to fuel this fire they've started."

I nodded. "What should I do about my mission? We haven't reported to Sabnack yet, but I am sure he'll be thrilled about this turn of events."

Judas let a smug chuckle escape his lips.

"I'm sure you're right. Not even I foresaw a situation where military troops needed to restore order in a U.S. city. If this Marcella is allowed to continue on her current trajectory, the country could find itself spiraling into a civil war."

"Your mission is now to stop that from happening."

"Wait. What happened to not calling attention from The Council and following through on an assignment to solidify my position as an Agent? Aren't you worried about an investigation?"

"Yes." Judas steepled his fingers and tapped his bottom lip the way he always did when he was deep in thought. "In fact, the lack of any sort of investigation after your debacle with Simeon has me even more worried. I have to wonder if they're looking into things covertly. If so, it will be that much harder to hide the Denarii Division."

He paused, seeming to consider his own words, then took a deep breath and continued.

"That does not alter the fact that your situation has changed. Following through on a localized assignment was one thing. This could turn into a nationwide event that would affect millions. We cannot allow that to happen."

Judas walked around to his chair again and sat down as if to punctuate the fact that the matter had been settled.

"Let me worry about The Council. You find out who this Marcella is and find a way to stop her."

He paused to peer up at me as I stood to leave.

"Do not forget your position as a Denarii Agent. You are sworn to secrecy. If Sabnack orders you to support the actions of this uprising, it is your duty to at least appear to do just that. I will handle The Council, but do not give them reason to come sniffing around if you can help it."

I nodded. "Understood. Anything else before I go?" I was so anxious to leave it was all I could do to keep from running out the door before he had a chance to answer the question.

"Yes. Next time you come in here, clean up first. You smell like you slept in a chicken coop."

I ventured a sniff at my shirt and realized he was right. Spending the night in an enclosed area with Quack had done nothing for my personal hygiene.

"Check. I will do my best to stay away from chicken coops too. Thanks for the tip."

I rounded the corner and hit the door at a near run. Rabble rousers or no, the only thing I cared about was getting back to my apartment. If I didn't reconnect with Quack in the next few minutes, I might have a mental breakdown of my own.

CHAPTER TWENTY-SEVEN

I got off the elevator at a dead sprint, hurtling down the hall toward my apartments. A wayward Judas Agent stepped in front of me carrying an arm full of paperwork, and we collided in a shower of spreadsheets and manilla folders. Normally, I would have stopped to help. It was my fault, after all, but I didn't have time. I could only offer him a perfunctory wave by way of apology in the wake of his curses. I had to get to my apartment—to Quack. The sense that we could no longer be apart was so strong, so undeniable that I was willing to do anything to get back to him.

Every nerve, fiber, and cell in my body shrieked with need. Primal as the need for oxygen and twice as overwhelming. I would tear my own skin off to get to Quack if I had to. I ran down the hall, juking around two more Agents to avoid knocking them off their feet. I drew stares and muttered comments, but I was beyond the point of caring. I was almost beyond the use of doors. I could get there so much faster if I just punched through the wall—if I only had my Whip Crack. I sprinted past the entrance to the community locker room and yanked the door open to the apartments.

The place had been tailor made to sleep hundreds of snoring Agents. Each apartment, and even the hall area outside, was fairly soundproofed, but when I stopped at mine, I could still hear Quack blaring out a nonstop stream of duckly cries inside. The shadowed flailing form I saw through the tinted glass told me he was as anxious and upset as I was.

I didn't bother trying to climb up the small hand and footholds on the wall. My pod was about five feet off the floor, but I didn't need to get inside, I just needed to open the door. I yanked on the handle, and Quack rocketed out in a flurry of loose feathers and noise. He flapped and honked, beating me about the face, head, and shoulders like a drowning victim, until I reached up and got a hold of his body to calm him down.

His wings settled into something that felt almost like a hug around my head as I held him close to me, and I found myself trying to slow my own panicked breathing as well.

"What have you done to me?" Quack retracted his wings and settled into my arms. He was always heavier than I expected, but I did my best to hold him out so he could look me in the face. *"Don't ever leave me like that again. And I can't tell you how disgusted I am to mean every word of that. Why does being away from you feel like it's going to kill me? Are you some kind of duck pervert? Did you douse me with a love potion while I was sleeping? Whatever it is, cut it out. You're not my type."*

I smiled and let out a chuckle, more out of relief than anything else. "I'm sorry. This separation anxiety is all part of the soul binding. We can't be apart; although, I'm surprised we can't even leave one another for a few hours."

"Hours?" Quack ruffled his feathers and smoothed them back down again. *"I was shouting the second you closed the door. I can't believe you didn't hear me."*

I shook my head. "Our mental link must be limited to line of sight somehow, and the apartments are soundproofed. I was probably too far away to hear you quacking within the first couple of steps."

"I don't care about that," Quack snapped. *"I care about why I am calling for you in the first place. You smell like sour milk, can't swim, are allergic to rain, and you gluttonous, pink, meat seekers even eat my kind. Why do I feel the need to be nestled in your backpack all the time?"*

I took in a breath and tried to put on my most calming voice. I didn't think Quack would storm away. I wasn't even sure he had the capacity, given our little problem, but I wasn't willing to take the chance. I would do my best to calm him down and explain. It was the least I could do, considering he had no say in the life he was now bound to live.

"Our souls are connected." I winced, wishing I had a way to cushion the blow somehow but couldn't. "Alex, my partner, and a Voodoo Witch Doctor joined us together in order to save me. I was sick, and it was the only way to cure my condition. The other option was worse than death, literally. They had no choice, and you were in the wrong place at the wrong time. That's about it."

I crouched down to the floor and let Quack step off my hands to the thick burgundy carpet then stood back up to reach into the open door of my apartment again.

"I can promise you this. If there is a way to fix our ... condition, I'll do everything in my power to make it happen."

I pulled out the black backpack and crouched back down to where Quack sat looking up at me.

"I'm sorry you were saddled with this. It wasn't fair. But for now, I promise not to leave you again until we can find a way to make this better."

I opened the backpack and laid it down on the floor where Quack could walk in. He eyed it for a moment, then waddled inside.

"Well, at least I don't have to worry about flying south for the winter."

Quack's feet hit something that sounded like silverware jingling together. I tried to peek in past him, but Quack fluffed his feathers to block my view.

"What do you have in there?" I narrowed my eyes but didn't reach in to find it.

"Nothing." He clipped the word off so fast it meant there was definitely something, but I decided to leave him to his privacy. I had no idea where he could have picked it up, but if flatware brought him comfort, more power to him.

"Whatever. Tell you what. I promise if we ever get this figured out, I'll find you a nice golf course lake in Florida. For now, we need to find Alex. Seems like I'm on a roll pissing off my friends."

"Did you lock her in a tiny sleeping hole too?"

I cringed. "No, and for the record, I thought you would sleep while I was gone. Alex left all on her own."

"Lucky her."

I picked up the backpack and slung it over my shoulder again, suddenly thankful no one had come in while Quack was exposed. When I ran in, I had been too desperate to care. In hindsight, standing in the middle of The Judas Agency with a living ... anything ... would have made for a tough explanation.

"Yeah, well, now we need to find her. We have a real disaster to stop, and I can't do it without her help."

CHAPTER TWENTY-EIGHT

Alex wasn't in her cubicle, wandering the halls, or in the gym. I searched every nook, cranny, and hidey hole I could think of. I even peeked in on the secret room she had shown me a while back, thinking maybe she had hidden herself away in there, but that had come up empty too. That led me to one last ditch idea. It probably should have been one of the first places I thought of.

I opened the door to Hula Harry's, and there, sitting alone on one of Dan's anti-ergonomic bar stools, sat my blue-haired, tattooed partner. She was hunched over a half drank glass of soda and three other glasses of various shapes and sizes, all festooned with different umbrellas, colorful fruits, and fancy straws. One even looked like it had a burnt-out sparkler lodged among the artful conglomeration.

Alex glanced over her shoulder to see me walk in, then promptly turned her back on me. Yup, this was going to be a peach conversation for sure.

I sat down on the stool next to her and smiled at Dan. "Can I have a Coke?"

"Only if you drink it somewhere else," Alex answered before Dan could. "That seat is taken."

Dan held his hands up. "I think I'll leave you two alone to chat and come back around a little later."

He walked away, and I turned my attention to Alex.

"This stool is taken by whom?"

"By me." Alex turned a dangerous eye in my direction. "Get up or I'll make you get up."

I turned toward the bar and set my feet firmly on the ground. "You might be able to pull me off this stool, but I am not leaving until we talk this out. What is your problem? Since when do you stomp away without saying where you're going or what you're planning to do?"

"Since my partner became a hypocrite and refused to back me. How is it that even when I want to do the right thing, you still throw up roadblocks? Is it ego or just an irritating compulsion to do the opposite of whatever I suggest?"

"There's more truth to that last part than I'd like to admit." I sighed and let out a humorless laugh. "But not this time. I am your partner, and I do have your back. I always have your back, and sometimes that means keeping you from doing things that aren't so smart."

Alex glared at me again. "So, you think I make stupid decisions? That my priorities are all screwed up? Maybe you're right, but that all stops now."

"Stops how? By stomping back to The Judas Agency to tell them where they can stick it if they don't like you interfering with their war? That will do nothing but get you thrown out on your ear."

Alex turned her eyes back to the bar, but she didn't say anything. I watched her for a minute, waiting for an answer until I realized she had already given me one.

"That's what you want isn't it? You want them to kick you

out, so you don't have to wrestle with your conscience anymore."

It wasn't a question so much as a statement.

"So, what if I do? At least I wouldn't have to carry out their crummy missions anymore."

Alex lifted her glass, took a swig of her soda, and slammed it to the bar again.

"And I wouldn't have a partner."

I leaned in until she met my eyes, and I held her gaze. "A partner with a conscience. Yes, it sucks to carry out their missions, but you are also in a position most Woebegone could only dream of." I put my hand on her arm. "You are a Judas Agent. You can go Topside, have access to their super inter-web thingy, and can pick locks and hotwire cars with your Android phone—which I still haven't seen turn into a robot, by the way. You have the resources to do damage control and stop the very worst of these atrocities from happening. How can you walk away from a responsibility like that?"

The irony of my pep talk did not escape me. How many times had Judas told me the same things? Granted, he had done it with a bit more venom, spit, and bulging forehead veins, but the point was still the same. Use your position to do good and don't get caught doing it. The only difference between me and Alex was the Denarius coin that would suck me into a void of nothingness if I revealed my true position as a double agent. I would have to tread carefully but tread I would.

Alex let her gaze fall to the line of adorned glasses in front of her. "Dan has a real knack for creating horrible drinks. This last one tasted like turpentine and honey served in a gym sock. I still can't get the smell out of my nose."

I laughed. "Listen to me. You can't quit. You are my partner." I reached over and took her hand, drawing her eyes up to mine. "I need you. I don't want to carry out the Judas missions any more than you do, but maybe together, we can find a way to minimize the death and destruction they can cause. We can be a secret duo working in the shadows."

"Like double agents."

I cringed inwardly at the description.

"Let's just call it damage control. Besides, you're the only one who can hear Quack. I hope you don't think I'm going to suffer that little gift all by myself."

She smiled but didn't let go of my hand.

"I heard that." I felt a rustle then saw Quack pop his head out of the pack just over my shoulder. *"This is the thanks I get for trying to give you some privacy."*

"What privacy?" I said. "You were listening to every word."

"Yes, but I was pretending not to hear every word. That's almost the same thing."

Alex snorted out a laugh.

I smiled back at her. "I'm glad you think he's funny."

"Anything that annoys you is hilarious."

I chuckled again, and we both stared at the wall for a few seconds in silence.

"So, are we good?" I said. "I only ask because we are in somewhat of a time crunch with this whole civil war thing."

Alex looked at me, sighed, and squeezed my hand before letting go. "We're good—for now. What's your next step? Now that telling Sabnack to shove his job isn't a plan anymore, I'm out of ideas."

"I'm pretty sure telling Sabnack to shove anything is a recipe for ritual suicide."

Alex laughed. "Okay, so what then?"

"First, we really do need to pay Sabnack a visit. We haven't given him a report in eons, and no matter what we're doing, we have to keep up appearances with him."

"I'll take care of that. Every time you talk to him, it makes him want to eat you."

I nodded. "And I even brought him Twizzlers."

Alex chuckled. "Then what? Taking orders from Sabnack is not going to help us stop what's going on Topside."

"Why don't you go back to that lovely cubicle heaven and start digging on that computer of yours. There has to be something about this Marcella. With all the contact the gang members have had with her, one of them must have carried a phone close enough to get a voice print or a video. Anything would help."

"And what are you going to do?"

I glanced at Quack over my shoulder. "We need to go back up and pay a visit to Medjine. Our bond is a little more … volatile than either of us would like. I need to see if there is anything we can do. It isn't fair to Quack to keep him in this bond if I can help it. Plus, I haven't forgotten about Ryan. MiRACL may have moved their operation to the UK, but their home base is still in Denver. I want to poke my nose in there and see what they're up to. Maybe I can get a line on Simeon. Medjine may even have some ideas on how we can evict him from Ryan's body."

Alex nodded. "I can't believe I am going to agree with you, but I think that's a good idea. I will see what I can dig up on reversing a Woebegone possession as well. We can meet back at The Agency later and compare notes."

I pointed at Alex's collar and cleared my throat.

Alex rolled her eyes and removed the lapel pin all Judas Agents carried. All Judas Agents but me. The pin gave us access to the Envisage Splice elevators, so we could travel Topside. Judas had taken mine as a punishment for botching too many of my assignments, and I had, in turn, stolen the one Alex wore so I could carry out a mission of my own. When she discovered hers was missing, I wanted to come clean, but somehow, she had believed I had given her my pin out of a grand gesture of generosity and friendship in order to keep her from getting into trouble. I hadn't corrected her. It would, no doubt, come back to bite me someday, but for now, I needed to borrow her ... my ... the pin to go Topside alone on this trip.

"All you have to do is ask. It's yours anyway."

I let out an uncomfortable laugh but didn't say anything else on the subject. "Thanks. I'll return it the second I get back."

Alex nodded. "You have enough room on that wonder-trike for two?"

"As long as you don't mind riding in the basket. I'm happy to share my sweet wheels with you anytime." I smiled, glad to have my partner back and even more glad she no longer wanted to use me as a punching bag.

Alex stood and we waved to Dan on the way out of the bar. He was just putting the finishing touches on a pair of flower adorned cocktails. He held them up as if to tempt us back with the sight of them.

"Next time," I said. Alex had already double-timed it to the door. "We have to go. Give it a try on these guys."

I motioned to a pair of Woebegone sitting at a nearby table. They looked at me, then at Dan, their eyes going so wide you would have thought he had leveled a shotgun at them.

"Good luck guys. You're going to need it."

CHAPTER TWENTY-NINE

The Envisage Splice-evator tossed me out in an alley not far from Medjine's Voodoo shop back in Denver. I was getting better at my landings. Yes, my feet were mired in an overturned trashcan full of leftover Chinese food and old newspapers, but I had missed the open dumpster not ten feet away. I would call that a definite win. Anytime I didn't have to climb out of a steaming sea of diapers was a good day in my book.

I shook off the remnants of Moo Goo Gai Pan and made my way to the street. I figured I would head to Medjine first then make my way to MiRACL headquarters. I wasn't sure what I would find there, but it had been far too long since we poked that nest. My soul leakage problem might have delayed me from helping Ryan, but I was not about to abandon him. If there was a way to boot Simeon out of his body, I planned to find it. And right now, Medjine was my best bet for signing his eviction papers.

I strolled out to the street and saw, much to my surprise, that everything looked peaceful. No anarchy, insanity, or confusion to be found. It wasn't L.A., but there had been riots everywhere. There was an overturned car, remnants of fires, and boarded up storefronts where rioters had broken out windows, but aside from that, everything was quiet.

I never understood why demonstrators destroyed their own city in protest of a cause. It was like burning down your house because it sucked to go to the DMV. It didn't make any sense. Ruining a local deli had nothing to do with sticking it to MiRACL and their cutting-edge medical breakthroughs. It was nothing but veiled hate and pointless violence.

I was, however, surprised to see the huge crowd of people who seemed to be wandering the aftermath.

"Wow. What's going on around here?" Quack poked his head out of his backpack and peeked over my shoulder as I turned up the street to head for Medjine's shop. *"Are they having one of those noise fests with the stage and all the screaming?"*

"You mean a concert?"

"Whatever. You people sit around throwing trash into the water and wading into my lake with your gross, pink bodies while some guy screams into a noise stick. And you think a goose migration is bad."

"On behalf of all gross, pink bodies everywhere, please accept my apology. No one should throw trash into a lake ... or wade in front of ducks naked."

"It wasn't so bad. They threw a lot of food out with that trash. As long as you stayed away from the plastic rings, it was like a duck smorgasbord."

"Well, it looks like you ate pretty well. I'm glad you enjoyed it."

"I feel like you hid an insult in there somewhere, but I don't want to think that hard. Are we almost to the moo-moo shop?"

"It's a Voodoo shop. Two totally different things, and yes, we are. It's just around the corner."

I watched the people on the street as I walked and got ready to turn up the alley to Medjine's place, but I couldn't shake the feeling that something felt odd. The people loitering on the street weren't doing anything wrong. They didn't even look all that out of place, but something was off. Then it hit me. No one moved ... not with a purpose anyway. No one talked or chatted on their cell phones. They all sort of wandered around in the eerie quiet with blank expressions on their faces, but no one seemed to be going anywhere. Everyone from business executives in tailored suits to homeless people in stained t-shirts and flip flops meandered the sidewalk together. It was as if they were waiting for something, but what?

As I surveyed the crowd even closer, I noticed something else. Everyone had something in their hand. They did not brandish their items as conventional weapons, but the more I looked, I recognized them as weapons, nonetheless. One had a broomstick, another carried a five-pound dumbbell, still another had a pair of wrenches held down at his side. It was like the world's weirdest remake of West Side Story. I kept scanning the street, trying to spot what they were waiting for or watching, but my eyes always slid back to the people. I didn't know why, but it was almost as if I couldn't look at the street. My gaze would go there and then slip off before I could focus on anything important.

And that's when things really got weird.

A rumble and a hiss caught my attention at the top of the block, and I turned to see a caravan of RTD buses rolling in our direction. As soon as they came into view, the crowd seemed to come alive, looking on toward the upcoming transports. Everyone turned to face the street as the buses arrived and pulled up to the curb. Through the windows, I saw several gang members dispersed on each bus. As soon as the doors opened, the people clambered to climb aboard. The crowd that had been so docile a few seconds ago became downright aggressive, shouting curses, and shoving one another out of the way. It was like someone had flipped an asshole switch and turned on the worst part in all of them.

"Okay." Quack piped in, disrupting my astonishment. *"I admit I'm not all that familiar with human behavior, but this is creeping me out more than that time all those kids camped out with their friend in the hockey mask."*

"This is definitely a twelve on the creep factor," I agreed. "Where do you think they're going?"

"I don't know, but I know where I don't want to go. I vote we stick to the sidewalk and stay off the rolling mass-murder box."

I nodded, but I knew we had to get on that bus and see where this was going.

A man in a yellow plaid shirt and face tattoos leaned out one of the tall folding doors and looked at me.

"You coming?"

I hesitated only a second, then stepped up and squeezed onto the bus, doing my best not to turn Quack into a duck pancake in the process.

CHAPTER THIRTY

When you're crammed onto a bus with every foot, butt, and armpit in your face, every mile feels like a millennium. Sweaty skin and dirty fabric mushed into me from every side, and the smell of so many bodies in one place reminded me of drowning without the use of water. The only thing missing from the sardine throng was sound. Once all the people made it onto the bus, everyone went back to their zombie, vegetative state—waiting, not talking or asking questions. Just fuel for whatever event was about to happen. I had no idea what the event could be, but the longer I waited, the more I became convinced that Quack and I had found our way into the middle of a ticking bomb.

I managed to wedge my back into a corner, so Quack had a little room to breathe, but we were crammed into the bus the way Vienna Sausages were stacked into a can.

"I am beginning to think you are not the best decision maker." Quack popped his head out over my shoulder. I was about to tell him he should stay down, but no one seemed to notice.

Quack stretched his little duck neck out and bit me on the ear. It felt like a pinch from a sumo wrestling crab claw.

"*Ouch.*" I thought in my head, not wanting to call more attention to myself than I had to. "*What was that for?*"

"*You have me crushed into a corner of a hot, smelly, moving metal box full of creepy people. I don't know what's about to happen, but whatever it is, I doubt I'll have time to bite you for it later. I figured I had better do it now and get it out of the way.*"

I reached up and rubbed my ear then checked my fingers for blood.

"*Oh, calm down,*" Quack said. "*Ducks don't have teeth. I couldn't pierce that leathery pink cover if I wanted to.*"

"*You know some ducks are pink under all those feathers too.*"

"*Not me, I checked. I am ebony through and through. I bet my blood is even darker than yours.*"

"*We can find out right now if you want to.*"

Clever as our cerebral conversation was, we were cut short when the bus came to a halt a few miles outside of the city. I stood closest to the door, so when it opened, I stepped out and off to the side as fast as I could to avoid being trampled by the mob of disembarking passengers. As soon as I was off, I made my way toward the back end of the bus, then swung my backpack off of my shoulders.

"I don't know what's going to happen, but you might want to get airborne. You can always swing back down and ride with me again once everything is clear."

I upended the backpack, thinking Quack would tumble out alone, but as his webbed little feet hit the ground, a whole plethora of other items rained down with him. Keys, pens, a small wrench, a pair of eyeglasses, coins, and a Zippo lighter.

If Quack could blush, I was pretty sure he would be doing it now.

"What is all this?"

"*I can't help it,*" he blurted out. "*I like shiny things. Certain items just call out to me, and I have to take them. I don't know why.*"

My old nest looked like a jewel studded hollow, only with junk instead of diamonds. I miss it so much."

"Great. I have a kleptomaniac duck as a partner."

"Hey, I didn't ask for this gig."

I started to shove stuff back into the pack then noticed something in my pocket as well. I reached inside and found a small, shiny, chrome-handled flashlight.

"Seriously?"

Quack held up his wings. *"Wasn't me I swear. I don't have thumbs, remember? I can't even turn that thing on."*

I was about to ask how he had managed to slip it into my pocket when a boom shook the ground. I turned to look toward the source of the noise, and my eyes went wide. The building across the street billowed smoke from the front doors, or at least from where the front doors had been. The doors themselves were now hanging in a mangled mess on either side of the smoldering opening where a stream of bizarrely armed people now rushed in.

I scanned the area looking for a sign or address, anything that would tell me why we were here, then I saw it. Across the street from where we had parked sat a WWII era tank, underneath was printed the words: Army National Guard Armory.

"Quack, get in the air right now. Fly high and stay clear. This is going to get ugly."

Quack didn't argue. He took a couple of steps, flapped his wings, and off he went. As soon as he was out of the way, I turned my attention back to the building at hand. It was a huge, single-story brick structure with few doors and almost no windows to speak of. I didn't see any guards on the outside. Of course, that didn't mean there weren't any inside the building, but considering the rate at which people were now pouring into the doors, they would be overtaken in a matter of minutes. When a wave of people flooded in without fear, there was only so much a few guns could do.

Almost two hundred people waited outside the building to form their second wave of attack, so I decided to focus my attention there. If I could find a way to stop that second wave from going in, even if I could delay them, maybe some of the people inside would have a chance to escape or fight back. It was worth a shot.

There were several power lines overhead. Not much use in and of themselves, but they were strung up there by steel poles. Those I might be able to work with.

Considering I had just been healed of a horrific affliction caused by overuse of my Topside powers, I was not all that eager to use them again, but the people inside needed a chance. Without me they had none.

I hurried over and placed my hands on the side of the post closest to the invading horde. I hesitated and looked down at my healed hands as my heart pounded in my chest. I had to do this, whatever the cost. I would deal with the consequences later. I took a deep breath and poured my will into my hands. The metal began to rust almost instantly.

Overuse or not, my power had grown by leaps and bounds. When I had started, I couldn't do much more than leave a dusty handprint on a piece of metal, now I could eat through steel the way water eroded sand. The metal crumbled under my fingers in seconds, and the towering power pole began to tumble.

It seemed to move slowly at first, but then the goliath gained speed as it toppled toward the ground. I ran away from the base to avoid the recoil. Someone screamed in the crowd of invaders, and everyone scattered among the sudden pop and snap of broken power lines.

When I had retreated far enough away, I turned to see the pole hit the ground. Everything around me shook, including the earth beneath my feet. My felled poll had landed in the perfect spot. Live power lines now blocked the building, and there was no obvious way to navigate past them. The invaders were still scattered about the area, but they didn't seem shaken in the least by my makeshift barricade. Once they were out of the way, they all seemed to regroup and take up that standby zombie mode again, as if they were waiting for new orders now that their original plan was no good. If I didn't know any better, I would swear this was some sort of alien body snatcher invasion. Considering some of the things I had seen lately, body snatching might not be out of the question. Either way, I hoped my little diversion was enough to allow anyone inside time to regroup and escape.

I stood by for a few more minutes, but it became clear that there was no way I could stop this attack. That left only one thing for me to do. Return to The Agency, regroup, and report what I had seen. Alex and I needed to go on the offensive. I was done watching all of this go down from the sidelines.

I surveyed the area, wondering how I could backtrack to my Splice point. I hadn't thought that through during my impulsive jump onto the bus. Quack might be right. My decision-making abilities could use some work.

I looked around for a car to steal, but I didn't have Alex or her fancy Android car hack to hotwire it. Then it hit me. I turned and marched right back onto the now empty bus. The engine was still running, and the seat was still warm. A ready-made escape mobile if I ever saw one.

I released the air brakes with a loud hiss, punched the D on the transmission selector, and off I went. Just like driving my old Maverick ... if it were shaped like a giant shoebox and filled with plastic seats. I'd be back to my Splice point in no time. Too bad I couldn't take the people in that building with me. I glanced down at my hands on the wheel and wondered if I would see any cracking. I had no idea how much power I would have to expel to damage my soul again, but it was worth it if some of those people got out. I'd just have to hope Quack's soul glue was stronger than mine.

No sooner had I thought of my feathered companion than he appeared. Quack must have been watching me from above because he performed an amazing aerial maneuver and flew in through an open side window of the moving bus. Thoughts of all the times I had seen birds face plant it into glass ran through my mind, and I was happy he had chosen an open one.

"Well, that didn't take long. Are we going back home?" Quack settled into the seat behind me and made himself comfortable.

"If Alex and I can't figure out how to stop this angry mob, I have a feeling that Armory is only the beginning. We need to get back and figure out a—"

Before I could finish my sentence, something slammed the bus hard enough to make me swerve. I checked the mirrors for a car or a rogue rhinoceros. Nothing was there. I kept scanning, but even as I looked in the mirrors something broadsided us again.

"What's happening?" Quack stood up and flapped his wings to maintain his balance. *"Stop doing that."*

"Hard as it is to believe, it's not me. Something's hitting us from the outside, but I can't see what it is. Can you fly out and get a bird's eye view?"

"No way. Gliding in is one thing. I'm way too big to take off out of here. It would be a death sentence."

"We really need to talk about your diet."

Quack started to bite off a retort, but the unseen force hit us again, all but forcing me into a set of parked cars. I glanced out the window and had that same feeling I had back on the street downtown. That sense that I wasn't seeing something right in front of my face. I kept checking the mirrors and looking out the passenger side window, but every time I looked in that direction, my eyes seemed to slide away again. It was like I refused to see what was right there.

I gathered my resolve and turned my head to glare out the

passenger side window, determined not to look away. What I saw there was enough to make me wish I hadn't.

For the barest moment, I glimpsed our pursuer. A horse and rider dressed in crimson colored armor like I had never seen. Plated steel was strapped to his body, all battle scarred and worn. Even the horse had been outfitted with heavy armor, and the two of them together stood almost as tall as the bus. The rider seemed to have some sort of ragged, olive colored cape and wore a bone helmet and mask that obscured his face. It was the most terrifying vision I'd ever seen, and I had witnessed demons that roamed the very depths of hell.

The moment I saw him, the rider peeled off. I forced myself to stare in the mirror long enough to see him standing in the street. He seemed to watch us for a moment then turned to gallop back toward the Armory. Either he figured the bus was too big to bring down, or he had decided it just wasn't worth the trouble. Regardless, he probably needed to regain command of his makeshift troops, and I was happy to have him off our tail.

I turned my eyes back to the road. Sweat ran down my face, and I felt my hands gripping the steering wheel so tightly I wasn't sure I'd ever peel them off again.

This mess kept getting bigger and bigger. First the unification of the gangs, then this Marcella character who didn't seem to exist. Now there was an invisible armor-clad maniac riding through downtown Denver? That went way past some ambitious gangbanger with an agenda. That rider was something I had never seen before. If we didn't figure out his identity and how to beat him, Alex and I might find that we were up against an adversary even The Judas Agency wasn't equipped to fight.

CHAPTER THIRTY-ONE

"I'm sorry we couldn't make it to the Voodoo shop to talk to Medjine about our little problem." I sort of half-whispered, half-thought the words as I ran through the maze of cubicles toward where I hoped Alex would be working in her office. "I promise we'll go back as soon as we fix what's going on here."

I hadn't gotten to MiRACL either, which meant Ryan would have to wait as well. I was frustrated by all the roadblocks that seemed to appear every time I set out to help him, but this was more important. Simeon and his evil plans would have to remain on the back burner for now.

Quack rustled inside the backpack but stayed hidden. *"If I have to wait for you to solve every problem the featherless world comes up with, we're never going to get there. I think all that uncovered skin gives you brain damage."*

I let out a little laugh as I turned another corner and jogged down an endless set of grey workspaces.

"You may be right. Maybe we should turn the world over to the bears."

I heard Quack squawk inside the bag. *"That's even worse.*

Have you seen what those things do in a lake? They poop anywhere. I startled a bear in the bushes once, and he left a thirteen-yard trail of disgusting bear nastiness. I had to move. Plus, they eat enough fish to feed a thousand ducks. They make people seem like a model of self-restraint."

If I hadn't been in such a hurry, I would have stopped to regain control of my laughter. As it was, I was now loping flat-footed like an idiot, trying not to snort myself to death.

"I'm glad you find that so funny. We'll see if you're laughing next time one gets into your house and he uses your living room for a toilet."

I coughed out another laugh and then got myself under control.

"It's not just that. I would have loved to see you scare the crap out of a bear ... literally."

I did not have to see Quack to sense the hint of pride in his voice. *"Yeah, that part was awesome."*

When I got to Alex's cubicle, I had almost forgotten why I was in such a rush. The second I laid eyes on her panicked expression, everything came back in a rush of dread and emotion.

"Where have you been? Do you have any idea what's been happening over the last few hours?"

I had my mouth open to speak first, but she beat me to it. "Have you seen these attacks? It's like everyone has lost their minds."

I nodded. "I was there. Quack and I ran into the—" I hesitated at what to call it, "the assault force and wound up riding with them all the way to the Armory. I wanted to stop them, but there were just too many."

"Which Armory?"

"And you're not going to believe what else I saw ... Wait, what do you mean which Armory?"

Alex grabbed me by the collar and pulled me into her cubicle, so I could peer down at her computer screen. It showed multiple locations all seemingly under attack.

"Wait, when did this happen?"

"There have been attacks all over the country. It started at a military base in California, then like dominos, bases began to fall under attack, one-by-one. They were all assaulted by bands of civilians with gang leaders coordinating the attacks. The media isn't helping either. They're siding with the community, saying the public is tired of government bureaucracy and are only acting out as free citizens. The whole country is splitting into pro- and anti-government, and both sides are out for blood. I've never seen anything so insane in my entire life."

I shook my head as I stared at the screens. "How could this happen so fast? I can't believe ordinary people would be so willing to jump into senseless violence like this. If I hadn't seen it with my own eyes, I wouldn't believe it."

"Well, it's happening, and I don't see an end in sight. If things keep escalating at this rate, the U.S. will be in an all-out war within weeks."

I stared at the screen for a moment then remembered about my run-in with the horse and rider during our escape. I leaned down and scrutinized one of the video feeds, anxious to see if I could spot something, or rather not spot something, in the area where the battles had occurred.

After scanning the footage for a few seconds, I recognized what I was looking for. A spot where no camera seemed to record.

"Look there. See that spot just out of frame next to the guard gate in that video?"

Alex stared at the screen. "Yeah, so what? We don't have time for—"

"Just try to gain a clear view of it on another camera. I bet you won't be able to."

Alex tried a few different feeds and couldn't get a view of the area. "Okay, fine. So what does that prove?"

"When we were in Denver, I noticed something weird in the street. It was before everyone got on the buses or got to the base. It was like a blank space. A spot I couldn't look at. It happened again when we were at the base."

"Soooooo whaaaaaaat." Alex drew out the words, clearly getting impatient.

"When we made our escape on the bus, I only saw it for a second but—"

I paused, realizing how ridiculous my story sounded.

"I swear if you don't finish that sentence, I am going to pull it out of your little toe."

"Okay." I blurted out the word like it pained me to say it. "I saw a horse and rider. They were all done up in super heavy armor, and the guy wore a bone mask and helmet of some kind. I know it sounds crazy, but if I didn't force myself to stare directly at them, I couldn't see them at all. It was like my eyes would look everywhere but the place where the rider was."

Alex stared at me for a minute with a deadpan expression on her face. "Are you telling me an invisible knight out of the dark ages chased you down in a public transportation bus?"

"And tried to run us off the road, yes. He hit us several times. It was like getting broadsided by a minivan."

"And you couldn't see it, until you could see it. Then it disappeared again? You're right, I'm sorry I asked."

I spun Alex around and pointed at the screen again. "Look at that spot on the video. I'll bet no matter how many cameras or cellphones you access, you will never get a good look at that spot in the landscape. That's because that ... thing is right there. I'll also bet that there is a spot like that in every single place where an attack occurred. I think that rider is controlling the people somehow. Making them aggressive and susceptible to suggestion. At least a suggestion to kill. Do you have a better theory as to why Johnny Good and Suzie Home Maker are suddenly willing to commit mass murder?"

Alex continued to stare at the screen. I could see that she wasn't quite buying into my story, but she didn't have a better theory either. "So how is this rider in so many places at once? These attacks occurred all over the country."

I shrugged. "Maybe he can travel super-fast. Almost instantly, the way we can with the Envisage Splice Transporter. You said the attacks happened one after the other, not at the same time. What if this rider traveled from one to the other, leading the attacks one by one?"

As I waited for her to process my less than rational theories, my mind went back to the only connection we had to this whole mess.

"I think we need to go back up and find this Marcella character and force her into explaining what is going on. Did you dig anything up on her while I was gone?"

Alex flashed me a glare that melted almost as fast into an expression of utter defeat.

"No. I searched everything I could think of. Either Marcella doesn't exist, or she is way better than we are at hiding her tracks."

We sat there for a minute, staring at her screen in frustration, then an idea hit me. It was a long shot, but at this point, long shots were all we had.

"What if this Marcella is a Niner like us?"

Alex shook her head and began to protest, but I held up a hand to stop her.

"She knows about our weaknesses, can somehow avoid detection from your super snooper computer. Maybe she's one of us."

Alex let out a breath in exasperation. "So, what if she is? That doesn't get us any closer to finding Marcella."

"No, but it just so happens I know an angel who likes to keep tabs on wayward souls who wander Topside. I think it's time we paid her a visit to find out what she really knows."

CHAPTER THIRTY-TWO

"So, what are we supposed to do?" Alex threw out her arms in exasperation. "Just wander around this park until Sammy, the Wonder Angel, shows up to stalk us?"

We had been walking around Echo Lake Park in the middle of Los Angeles for several hours, hoping that Sammy would do just that. It was a frustrating plan, but Quack didn't seem to mind. He had been paddling around the nearby lake since we arrived. The moment he laid eyes on it, he took off like a preteen at a water park on the first day of summer. I wasn't sure I would ever get him out again.

I let out an exasperated breath of my own. "If you have any other ideas, I'm happy to hear them. It's not like we have her phone number. I'll bet she doesn't even have a phone."

"Who needs one when you can track everyone you want to talk to and show up like annoying in-laws?"

We walked around a dirt path that circled the lake. As stakeouts went, this one was pretty good. Sunshine, sixty degrees, grass, and blue skies. Way better than a smelly sedan and three-day old Chinese food.

"I know we're in a time crunch, but let's try to enjoy it up here. How often do Niners get to stroll through a park?"

Alex grumbled. "I know, but every second we spend having a good time is another second people out there could be dying. That sort of spoils the ambiance."

I nodded. "Sammy will show. I can feel it."

To be honest, I couldn't feel anything. The last few times she had appeared, Alex had been less than hospitable. I just hoped she was the type of angel who couldn't take a hint.

A trio of military choppers flew by overhead, buffeting the air like rapid fire machine guns. We watched them go by, then as if to prove my point, Alex raised her chin toward the sky and shouted as if in accusation.

"Hey! If you're watching, or tracking, or whatever it is you do, fly your feathery butt down here. We need to talk to you."

Alex stopped and put her hands on her hips, surveying the park for any sign of Sammy.

"That'll bring her running." I stopped next to her and looked out at the lake, keeping my eye on Quack. "Either that or someone out here will call the cops, and you'll get to see what it's like to visit a mental ward."

"This is stupid." Alex started to walk again, this time at a pace that was more storming march than casual stroll. "I'll bet she'd pop up if we shot up a mini-mall."

"Whoa, where did that come from? I thought we were trying to help people not—"

"I just mean she only seems to be interested if we're getting into trouble. What kind of angel only shows up when we're about to wreak havoc and then stands back to watch like some weird peeping Tom?"

"It is a frustrating conundrum." The voice cut in from behind us. Way too close and loud enough to make us both jump out of our shoes.

Alex and I spun into a defensive position, flanking the path and our new guest. Sammy stood between us looking as oblivious to her untimely actions as always.

"What a beautiful day for a walk." Sammy smiled, ignoring our readied fists. "Are you two up for a new mission or just taking a stroll in the land of the living?"

"Actually, we're looking for you." I straightened and dropped my hands before Alex could lash out a response. "Thanks for coming."

Sammy put her hands on her chest and looked from Alex to me again. Alex had lowered her arms to her sides again, but I noticed her hands were still balled into fists. I would have to take the lead in the conversation if we wanted any diplomatic chance of getting the information we needed.

"Me? I thought you two were angry about the whole ..."

Sammy winced and made a nondescript motion with her hand.

"The dog on a leash thing?" Alex finished the sentence for her. "Yeah, we haven't forgotten about that."

I held out a hand as if to tell her to stay calm. We weren't here to hash out our privacy policies. We needed information.

"Actually, we wanted to talk to you about that," I said. "Not us, but we wanted to know how your tracking talent works and whether you track anyone besides us?"

For the first time since we had met her, Sammy betrayed a narrow-eyed look of suspicion. "What do you mean, anyone besides you?"

Alex stepped around next to me and eyed her back. "We mean are there any other Niners you keep tabs on? Specifically, one known as Marcella?"

Sammy took a step back and held her hands out in front of her.

"I told you, I can't interfere with Earthly affairs. I've already helped you way more than I should have. I'm sorry but—"

Alex matched her step for step.

"Listen, this Marcella is not a part of your Earthly affairs edict. If you are tracking her, that means she is from somewhere other than here, so telling us where she is does not break your rule. She is meddling in things that are going to kill thousands of people, maybe more ... much more. We just want to know how to find her. You don't have to do anything after that."

Alex had gotten so close to Sammy that it would have been tough to slip a sheet of typing paper between them. I put a hand on Alex's shoulder and eased her back a few inches to allow Sammy room to breathe.

For a moment, she didn't say anything at all, she just stood there looking from Alex to me and back to Alex again. There was no fear in her eyes, only contemplation, like when someone is trying to plan their next chess move. In truth, we had nothing. Sammy could transform into her pigeon form and fly away or even strike us down with her flaming sword. All we could do was hope the angel inside of her would come through and help humanity rather than follow some stupid rule.

"Strictly speaking, it is against my mandate to track any otherworldly entities unless I am acting in an official capacity. If I were tracking someone outside of that mandate, it would be against the rules set out to guide me in my position."

"But you are tracking us." I tilted my head and stared at her. "Isn't that outside of your mandate?"

"Well, yes, but we're all friends."

My arm shot out to grab Alex's wrist before she could launch into an unproductive tirade.

"All right, so as friends, can you tell us where this Marcella is?"

Sammy sighed. And backed away from us a few steps.

"Please understand. Any direct involvement I have in the affairs of—"

"Yes, we heard you the first time." Alex stepped forward but didn't close the distance the way she had before. Something had changed in her demeanor. She no longer seemed angry. Her eyes had softened into pleading, and her voice was calm. "That does not change the fact that you are our only hope. We need your help."

I stepped up next to Alex and put a hand on her shoulder.

"She's right. I understand what we're asking you to do but think about what we've entrusted with you. Alex and I are Judas Agents. Saving people is not what we do. If our superiors find out what we're up to ..."

I let the thought trail off, so she could finish the mental image herself.

"We are all coloring outside the lines here," I continued. "We're just asking for a location. A place where we can go talk to her. You don't have to be involved any more than that."

Sammy looked at us for a moment longer then sighed.

"I don't know an exact location. I tracked her when she arrived Topside, but she's found a way to block my efforts to keep tabs on her."

Our shoulders fell, and Alex closed her eyes. I could tell she was doing her best to control her frustration and anger, but it was only a matter of moments before she erupted in a fury.

"I do know where she has based her operations out of though."

We both locked eyes with Sammy.

"What do you mean?" I tried to hold back my expectation but couldn't help but take a step in her direction.

"She has a base of operations in a city maintenance compound." Sammy produced a piece of paper and a pen from her coat pocket and began scrawling out an address. "The place has been shut down since the riots. They took it over, and Marcella works out off an office in one of the maintenance buildings."

She offered me the paper, and I realized my mouth hung half open. I blinked several times, shut my mouth, and took the scrap of paper. "Thank you, Sammy. You've done the right thing, I promise."

"Don't thank me just yet," she said. "That place will be crawling with guards, and they will not be happy to see the two of you. Give them the code phrase, 'Dark Sunrise.' That should gain you safe passage in to talk to her."

Alex nodded. "Thank you. We won't share how we found them. I promise you that."

Sammy nodded back. "Just don't get yourselves hurt. I sort of like seeing you around, even if you don't like it when I show up."

That stung a little, and I could see that it had punched Alex in the gut too.

"We still need to talk about this tracking issue," she said, "but you're not all that bad to have around. Let's just figure this thing out with Marcella, then we can work out visitation rights."

Sammy chuckled and answered with a nod.

"Let's go," I said. "I want to talk to Marcella before she has a chance to do any more damage."

We waved goodbye to Sammy and headed out of the park. All I had to do now was reel in my duck, and we could be off to meet the mystery woman bent on driving the country into death and ruin.

CHAPTER THIRTY-THREE

We walked up to the outer gates of the maintenance compound to find a single worker sitting just inside the barbed wire capped fence. He sat on an old folding chair wearing olive colored coveralls, a greasy reflective vest, and a yellowish hardhat that looked like it had seen more than its fair share of cranium denting collisions. He barely glanced up from his newspaper as we approached then went back to whatever article he read as if he had never seen us at all.

I did my best to ignore his discourtesy and put on a friendly smile as we approached the locked gate.

"Sorry to bother you. We're looking for someone who is supposed to be working out of the buildings in there." I pointed to the half dozen or so metal structures behind him. "We'd like to chat with the person in charge."

Hard Hat never even glanced up from his news article. He just went on reading as if he hadn't heard a word I said.

I stepped in close to the gate and wrapped my hand into the chain link. "Marcella. Does that name ring a bell?"

That piqued his interest enough to raise an eyebrow, and this time, he looked up at me.

"We are here to see Marcella. We have an appointment at Dark Sunrise."

He eyed me up and down then did the same to Alex.

"What do you want with Marcella?"

Alex showed her teeth in the unfriendliest of smiles. "If we were here to talk to a gate stooge, we would have asked to talk to you. My partner said we are here to talk to Marcella. Now open the gate unless you want us to open it for you."

Hard Hat sniffed then made a methodical show of folding his newspaper before getting up to unlock the heavy padlock. He pulled the chain through and opened the gate with a loud creak, ushering us in.

"Second building on the left," he said. "If I were you, I'd go in chanting that passphrase. The guys in there aren't as friendly as I am."

I shot him a sneer and nodded as we walked by. "Thanks for the tip."

I noted the fact that he locked the gate again, depositing the key into his pocket, as we made our way toward the building he had described.

"I hope this meeting goes well." I uttered out of the corner of my mouth. "If it doesn't, we are going to have a heck of a time getting out of here."

I glanced up to see another group of choppers fly by overhead, this time there were six of them. "Does that strike you as weird at all?"

"What?"

"All the helicopters. It's not like we're a M.A.S.H. unit in Vietnam. Why are there so many choppers flying around in L.A.?"

"Just worry about Marcella. If we have to fight our way out of here, I'm going to use her as my shield."

I nodded. "Good plan. Use the only person who can stop this mess as a bullet-proof vest."

"This was your bright idea. I just want a Plan B for when yours goes south."

"Oh, ye of little faith." I dropped my backpack next to the door as we walked into the building. "Don't forget about our cavalry. All we have to do is call—"

"What's Quack going to do if we get into trouble? Annoy them to death? They can't hear him talk, remember?"

"I heard that."

His voice sounded muffled from inside the backpack even though he spoke in our heads. That made no sense whatsoever, but I didn't have time to worry about that right now.

As we strode further into the building, I realized we were in some sort of vehicle maintenance shop. A large tractor sat in the rear of the huge bay, looking like it had seen its fair share of work around the grounds. It had an open cab and a big front-end loading bucket, presumably to fill the city trucks with whatever they needed to haul around the city. I had used one similar to it when I had been alive working at a junkyard, but this was no time to reminisce.

The vehicles that resided in the forefront of the bay were more important. The very sight of them was enough to make Alex and I both skid to a halt. Lined up in neat rows sat dozens of motorcycles, mostly Harleys, and almost all looked to have sustained some sort of damage. Perhaps from the bumper of a speeding van bent on escaping from a marauding gang of murderous bikers in a shipping yard.

Alex latched onto my arm so tight I thought she might squeeze it off as bikers began to ooze out of the woodwork like cockroaches. They seemed to come from everywhere—open doors, around corners, out from between the bikes—and all of them looked like they had just been introduced to the two people who had shot their grandmother.

"Dark Sunrise." I shouted out the words so loud they

echoed through the open bay of the shop. "Dark Sunrise. We're just here to talk. Dark Sunrise."

I couldn't seem to stop saying the phrase, as if it were a lonely piece of driftwood in a sea of crocodiles and sharks.

A man appeared to our left, looking nothing like the angry rabble closing in on us despite my continuous profession of the passphrase. He wore a dark business suit complete with shiny loafers and a bright blue tie. He had descended a set of stairs that led to an upper mezzanine and offered his hand by way of invitation.

"You are here to see Marcella?"

Alex and I nodded emphatically.

"Dark Sunrise." My voice cracked again.

"So you've said. Please, come this way."

I forced myself to shut my mouth and tried not to look like I wanted to sprint up the stairs and escape the gang on the bottom floor. If Alex hadn't walked up the stairs ahead of me, I'm not sure I would have been all that successful.

The thought of having to cross that sea of angry bikers in order to leave did not make me feel better about an escape. If we had to get out of here in a hurry, Alex and I were going to need more than a duck. We would need a miracle.

The mezzanine at the top of the stairs turned out to be less comforting than I had hoped. Constructed of steel grating, it allowed us a full view of the floor beneath, along with all the bikers glaring up at our feet. I noticed most of them had put down their tools and had taken up posts next to doors and windows. Most of them held one kind of water expelling device or another. Unlike the limited array they had carried on their bikes at the shipping yard, now they held everything from extinguishers to Super Soakers to weed sprayers.

Suit stopped us outside of a makeshift office, and we waited as he went inside then came out, trailing a woman wearing jeans and a t-shirt. She was tall with dark hair and skin and had an air of command about her. The perma-scowl on her face said she was not someone to mess with.

She walked onto the mezzanine to join us. There was just enough room to keep us at an unfriendly distance apart from one another. If Alex wanted to make a grab for her, it would take a few steps to do it and probably draw a sea of deadly spray from below.

"I don't know you. How did you come by the passcode to gain entry here?"

I nodded and tried to take a step forward, but her glance down at my feet told me any move in her direction would be unwise. "We have a mutual friend. You are Marcella?"

Scowl Commander raised her chin but didn't answer.

After a moment, Alex broke the silence. "We're not here to fight. We simply want a meeting with the leader of your forces."

"Anything you wish to say to her, you can say to me."

Alex let out a laugh that made my toes curl in panic.

"Your gate guard said the same thing. If we wanted to leave a message, we would've talked to him."

Tension in the room rose, and I heard the clack of biker boots ascending the metal stairwell behind us.

"Hold on." I raised my hands in placation. "We don't want any trouble. We're here to talk." I addressed the entire room then let my eyes fall back on the woman standing across from us. "But my partner is right. We're here to talk to the one who is in charge of your operation. If we're going to find a peaceful way out of this, we can't do it by—"

The room erupted in laughter, cutting me off, and I began to realize how big of a lion's den we had walked into.

"Take them to Pershing Square tomorrow." The voice came from a skinny biker to our left holding a Super Soaker squirt gun. "They can have their peace talk with Marcella out there."

Laughter re-erupted. Scowl Commander raised a hand, and the laugher stopped as more bikers appeared from around the corner of the office area, presumably from a second stairwell in the back. We were being surrounded, and soon, we would be the pride's main course.

"What makes you think we want peace?" Scowl Commander dared a step in our direction now that her biker guard had closed in around us. They had spread out along the rails, forming an impenetrable wall as their leader continued to speak. "Marcella does not take meetings, sit down for negotiations, or hold prisoners. She showed us how to rebuild this country, and we intend to do it. There is no place in our new nation for those like you."

Alex let out a chuckle. "You have no idea how right you are."

I turned a glare in her direction. "You're not helping here."

Alex shrugged. "We were never getting out of here the second we walked through that door."

I gaped.

"What? If I am going down, I'm not going to do it by kissing up to some lowlife gangbanger."

Hoses and nozzles raised in our direction.

"Hold on a second. There's always Plan B."

"What Plan B?" Alex motioned to the ring of water armed bikers surrounding us. "There is no Plan B."

"There is always a Plan B," I said it louder, enunciating every word. This time my declaration was met with a grouchy response.

"Hold your horses. I don't have any thumbs. I can only work so fast."

Alex turned her stunned gaze down toward the door where we had come in. The door where I had left Quack inside my backpack. With all the bikers advancing to the top of the mezzanine, it gave him time to climb out and implement our plan. Unfortunately, his flapping and duck grunts had drawn the attention of everyone else on the mezzanine as well.

"Is that a duck?" For the first time, I saw Scowl Commander's expression break. She didn't smile, but it definitely turned to a look of baffled confusion.

"Yes, it is," I exclaimed. "Let's see how you like trying to hit us with your water guns in the dark!"

I grabbed Alex and poised myself to run as Quack flapped his wings and used his webbed feet to flip the switch next to the door. Instead of concealing darkness, the fire alarms went off.

"No, Quack, not the red one, the other ... never mind." I groaned in defeat.

The bikers erupted in laughter again. Even Scowl Commander got a chuckle out of the debacle.

"I don't know how you trained a duck to do that, but it was a nice try," she said over the wailing alarm. "Now, I'm afraid it's over for you two."

I glanced down at Quack through the flashing strobes then nodded as I grabbed Alex and pulled her in close to me. She tensed in surprise, but I didn't let go. Then I poured all my Topside power down into my feet. "Thanks for the hospitality, but we really do have to go."

I glanced back to Alex and had just enough time to say, "Sorry about this."

The steel grating beneath our feet crumbled away to rust and dust as Quack found the right switch, and the lights went out for real. Alex and I careened down toward the lower floor disappearing into the darkness.

CHAPTER THIRTY-FOUR

We hit the ground running as the hiss of water spray went off above our heads. Alex and I made a break toward the exit, but I grabbed her arm and jerked her toward the darkness in the back of the maintenance shop as soon as I snagged the backpack laying by the door.

"What are you doing?" she yelled over the blaring fire alarm.

"Trust me. Those doors are locked, and even if they weren't, we would never get past the gate stooge outside."

Quack had doused all the lights in the building, but the flashing strobes that corresponded with the screeching fire alarm lit our way every few seconds. I could see that Alex had her Ruger at the ready, but I wasn't sure how much good it would do. Unless she had a clip with thirty rounds and hit everyone with the first shot, she wouldn't take down every biker in the place.

I clambered through the darkness, one hand out in front of me, one hand dragging Alex by her coat sleeve.

"I hope you're not planning to do what I think you're planning to do," she shouted.

When we climbed up onto the step of the old tractor she growled. "This is not a 77' Chevy. You are going to get us melted."

I jumped into the seat and fumbled my hand around the firewall until I found the ignition.

"We have about a half a second before they find us back here. I know how to drive this thing. Jump on. We're going out through that door." I nodded toward the tall vehicle access in front of the building.

Alex groaned again. "It's not like we have much choice left."

She leapt onto the tractor and stood on the running board next to me. I hit the ignition, and the engine roared to life. The throttle handle squeaked as I yanked it down, then I threw it in gear and popped the clutch. The tractor lurched forward so hard it tore my hands away from the steering wheel, and Alex almost went flying off the back.

I barely had time to reach forward again and fumble with the bucket controls. The front-end loader scraped along the floor for several feet, scooping bikes into the bucket before I got it into the air. The rest were plowed over by the blade or crushed under the tires in our rush to get to the door. We weren't making any friends in this biker community, that was for sure.

The one thing I hadn't taken into account in my escape plan was the fact that our path would take us right through the waiting crossfire of our rainwater death squad. Our getaway vehicle had an open cab and offered no protection against the oncoming liquid onslaught.

Alex threw the hood up on her coat and turned her back to the front line. I wanted to duck, but I was busy trying to simultaneously steer, raise the front-end loader, and avoid getting hung up on the labyrinth of downed motorcycles. The tractor engine screamed as we tore through the building, and I looked up just in time to see several bikers who still stood above us on the mezzanine.

As we passed beneath them, they let us have it with their Super Soakers and fire extinguishers. A few of them even fired handguns for good measure. Alex screamed and ducked her head, but I had no such protection. I wore my Gore-Tex outfit, so my body was covered, but my head and neck were exposed. I drove under the hail of rainwater and gunfire not knowing what else to do. I would heal from the bullets. But I had to hope I would either survive the water, or Alex would take over and drive once we made it past the deadly gauntlet and I was gone.

I braced for the inevitable. When I was sure my head was about to be turned to sludge, something else hit me. An awkward weight heavy enough to strain my neck but not part of the attack. It was actually soft like a pillow, if a pillow weighed ten pounds.

Quack landed square on my head and flapped his wings to maintain his balance. He took the water streaming down like a secret service agent taking a bullet for the president. He even braved quite a few bullets himself. I was glad the bikers had resigned themselves mostly to the use of rainwater rather than guns. Those who did shoot at us seemed to do so with the desperate accuracy of a last-ditch effort. Their shots went wide and missed not only us but the vulnerable waterfowl who sheltered my head as well.

The huge bucket on the front of the tractor smashed into the overhead door with a steel ripping crash, and all at once, we were outside. The jarring impact threatened to dislodge us from the tractor for a second time, but we held on. Quack launched off my head to fly in the air. I squinted at the sudden brightness then swung the tractor around to head straight for the gates where Hard Hat waited in his chair.

I aimed the tractor straight at him. Hard Hat threw his paper over his head and all but fell over backward trying to dive out of the way. I lowered the bucket to gate-ramming level and smiled. The bikers were on foot behind us since we had taken out their only modes of transportation ... again. They couldn't keep up with us for long. We had been in an impossible spot, but now we were home free.

I grinned despite myself and cast a glance over at Hard Hat as we sped by. I half expected him to draw a pistol and take a couple of shots at us on the way out, but he had done no such thing. In one hand he held a radio, and in the other, he had something else. At first, I couldn't tell what it was, but then my heart stopped as I recognized it. He held a thin hose connected to a nozzle. My eyes traced the line to a pressurized tank several feet behind him. I hadn't even noticed it before.

As we went by, I grabbed Alex and pulled her down again, making sure her hood was up over her head. I had no such protection. Quack would not be here for me a second time. I raised my arms in front of my face, doing my best to shield myself from the incoming water. As I turned to duck away, I felt it hit me in the back of the head and run down my neck and back. It was not a full-on strike, but likely a deflected stream off my arm. Regardless of how the splatter had happened, it was enough.

It felt like liquid fire running down my skin. I wanted to reach back and wipe the watery assault away, but I didn't dare touch it. Doing so would only spread the burning to my hands and arms.

I screamed, thankful that the throttle was not something I had to maintain on my own. It was wide open and would stay that way unless I shoved the handle back down. The tractor would keep running at full speed.

Alex stood up and grabbed the wheel, and I tore off my jacket and wet shirt to halt the acid-like burning.

"Gabe! Are you okay?" She continued to steer the tractor

from the sideboard, guiding it into the parking lot and toward the street. "Let me see."

I shook my head then shrieked at the pain from moving. Alex tried to throttle the tractor down, but I blocked her hand and pointed forward. "Just keep going. Get us to the Splice point. We need to get back to The Nine and regroup before they find a way to chase us and finish the job."

Alex scowled at me for a moment, but she complied. It would be a bumpy ride, and there would be no shortage of stares. But a ride on a tractor was faster than running, and I was in no shape for a jog. My neck and back felt like they had been peeled off with a rusty cheese grater then wrapped in jellyfish tentacles. It was all I could do to breathe through the pain and stay awake.

I just wanted to be back to the relative safety of The Agency. We had been fools to think we could reason with someone like Marcella and her ragtag army. We needed to get back and come up with a plan. One that would take her out of the equation for good.

CHAPTER THIRTY-FIVE

"Gabe, this is bad." Alex and I got back to The Judas Agency in almost one piece, thanks to our Bonnie and Clyde tractor run through the outskirts of the city. In truth, it hadn't been far to the Splice point, but the ride had been excruciating, considering my skin had been melted to a slimy goo.

"It would have been a lot worse if Quack hadn't taken that first shot for me."

I slumped forward on one of the locker room benches while Alex examined the damage on my head, neck, and back.

The three of us sequestered ourselves to the far corner, ensuring some measure of privacy. Quack still sat inside my backpack next to me, his head poking out of the top flap. If he could grin with pride, I was pretty sure he would have been smiling from tiny duck ear to tiny duck ear.

"*It was only water. I just did what any heroic, selfless duck would do.*"

I laughed. "It was water, but they shot bullets at us too. You risked your life for me." I reached out and patted Quack on the head. "Thank you."

Quack stretched his neck and beamed. "*I really saved your*

bacon out there. Don't forget about Plan B. If I hadn't distracted them with the lights, you wouldn't have gotten away."

My grin shrunk a bit at that. "Yeah, we need to work on the difference between a fire alarm and a light switch."

Quack scoffed. *"Whatever. I got the job done. Is there some kind of medal for bravery or staying calm under fire? I should get one of those, especially if it's shiny. Are your medals shiny?"*

I winced as Alex patted the wound on my back with a dry towel. "Do you have to do that?"

"Do I have to do this?" Her voice went up an octave.

Alex walked to a nearby shelf and retrieved a handheld mirror then came back to where I sat on my bench. She pulled me to my feet a little faster than necessary and looked me square in the eyes.

"That stunt almost got us killed. We let them lock us into a building full of rainwater, and your tractor escape wasn't much better."

"At least we made it out—"

"I know we got out, but it could have been so much worse." Her voice cracked. "If they had—"

She cut herself off and jerked me around to face the wall mirror.

I hissed at the pain. "Hey, easy."

Using her handheld version, she showed me the damage on my neck and back. She was right. It was bad.

All the skin had turned to a shriveled, wet mess, and most of it had dissolved away, exposing the damaged tissue underneath. The pain was bearable so long as no one touched it, or I didn't move ... or talk ... or breathe.

"What do you expect me to do with that? You aren't bleeding anymore, but you're oozing everywhere. You need to take care of this."

I shrugged and immediately regretted it.

"Does The Judas Agency have some sort of infirmary?"

Alex grimaced and answered with a sort of half shrug of her own. "Yes and no. We do have an infirmary, but they sort of figure the best way to heal major injuries is to recycle you through the Pools."

I recoiled. "What? That's terrible."

Alex put her mirror down and handed me my coat. "Just don't go wandering out of the building with one of their med techs. They don't like to make a mess in their office."

I stared at her for a minute, trying to decide if she was serious or not.

"Come on. I'll even buy you an ice cream if you're good."

Alex walked back, grabbed Quack in his backpack, and then started heading me toward the door. I was shirtless and still wore my Topside Gore-Tex pants. I carried my coat, but my shirt had gone into the closest ditch once it had been soaked with rainwater. So I didn't feel all that prepared to walk the halls of The Judas Agency.

"Hold on, at least let me change my pants and find another shirt."

"You're going to put a shirt on over that? I don't think so, not unless you want them to rip it off you when you get there."

I groaned and tried not to turn my head to look at her. "All right, but at least let me change into my jeans."

Alex sighed. "Fine but hurry up."

I smiled and walked over to the locker where I had stored my regular clothes. Alex hung back to give me a little privacy. I opened the door so I could change, only to have a whole new problem vibrate into the equation. The Denarius coin in my pocket began to buzz with its usual uncanny timing. Judas wanted to see me, and of course, it had to be right now.

I changed my pants as fast as I could and stopped by the community clothing bin to look for a shirt I could use when the infirmary murderers got done patching me up. I found a black hoodie that would work to cover my head as well.

When I walked back around the corner, I had the hoodie in my hand and what I hoped was a plausible excuse to get away for a little while.

"All set to see the doctor?"

I nodded and winced again. Alex still had the backpack with Quack, so I reached out to take it out of her hands.

"Why don't I head over there on my own? I hoped you could research something while they patch me up."

Alex narrowed her eyes at me in suspicion.

"I'm serious. Remember all those choppers flying by when we were at the maintenance compound?"

"Actually, I was a little busy trying not to die."

"Well, more than a few flew by ... military choppers. It happened when we were at the park too. The kind that transport troops."

Alex shook her head. "So what?"

"So, I'm just wondering what is going on. Is there any way you can do a little checking through your system? Is the U.S. moving troops to help with police? Maybe there's something we can use."

Alex stared at me for a minute then nodded her head. "Yeah, that should be easy enough to figure out. I don't know how we can use that against Marcella, but we should know all we can if we're going to put up any kind of fight against her."

I nodded. "I'll be trying to think of a plan while they are patching me up."

"The infirmary is back that way." She pointed toward the rear exit to the locker rooms. "It's on the third floor. You can't miss it."

Alex glanced down at my pack and smiled. "Don't jostle him too much, he's had a big day. I think he's asleep."

I opened the flap to the backpack and peeked inside. Sure enough, Quack had his head tucked under his wing, and he was sound asleep.

I couldn't help but smile. He had really saved me today. I was getting more than a little attached to him. Quack wasn't so bad once you got used to him. He just happened to have one of those personalities that could fill a room ... and overflow it out the windows.

"I'll meet you back in your office as soon as I'm done in the infirmary. And hey," I touched her arm. "I'm sorry. You know, about getting us into that mess."

"I know." She smiled. "I've gotten used to having you around. Let's try to keep it that way. Now go get yourself fixed up and don't be long." She made her way toward the front exit. "I don't want things to spin any more out of control while we sit on our hands."

I nodded in agreement, backing away to head in the other direction. "I'll be there before you can say 'psychotic gang war.'"

She turned and walked out the door, and I hurried on my way as well. Whatever they did in the infirmary, I hoped they did it fast. I talked a good game, but I could barely move. I needed to get up to Judas's office, and I couldn't do it in a shirtless mess. Managing to do both in time to keep Alex from getting suspicious would be nothing short of miraculous.

I sighed, already knowing I'd have to come up with another lie to cover my tracks. Even when we worked on the same side, honesty was impossible. Sometimes being the good guy sucked.

CHAPTER THIRTY-SIX

The infirmary medics turned out to be way more helpful than I thought they would be. It was a fact that put me on edge when I got there. I was convinced that they were only being nice in order to lure me into a gas chamber or firing squad somewhere, so I could be recycled instead of bandaged up and healed. In the end, they had done a great job of dressing my wounds.

They didn't offer any painkillers though. It might be an infirmary, but we were still in Hell.

When I stepped out of the elevator into Judas's waiting room, I headed straight for his office door. I wasn't in the mood to engage in the usual banter with his receptionist, and she didn't look like she was in the mood either. She just glanced at me over her horned-rimmed glasses and then waved me on. I had my new hoodie on with the hood up over my head to hide my first aid fashion accessories. It was hard to walk without doing a zombie impression, but I did my best to look natural despite the searing pain every move caused to my head, neck, and back. I had plenty to tell Judas but letting on about my injuries was not one of them. He would either take me out of the field or send me straight to the Pools to be reborn all pink, shiny, and new. I couldn't afford either one. Alex and I had a job to do, and we couldn't do it if I were out of the game altogether.

I was about halfway to his door when the receptionist's voice stopped me.

"That's a nice backpack you have there. Anything interesting inside?"

I stopped cold in my tracks. I couldn't believe I had been so stupid. I had taken to wearing the backpack low and loose to avoid my injuries, and I hadn't heard a peep out of Quack since I had been with Alex. That, combined with my pain and exhaustion, had made me forget Quack was even there. Something in the receptionist's tone told me I was not the only one who knew I had a hitchhiker along for the ride. Judas Iscariot's personal assistant had a superpower of her own. She seemed to know everything about everyone all the time. I didn't know how she did it. I had a theory that it had something to do with the never-ending pile of memos she always filed on her desk. Either way, I was guessing she knew about my new friend and maybe even why we were together. Of course, I could be wrong, but she was far too shrewd to let on that she knew. So, we were at a standoff.

I couldn't take Quack into the office with me because by doing so he would learn the true origin of my position as a Denarii Agent. Doing that would get me sucked right into the tortuous void of the coin—a deep, dark place reserved only for traitors to the cause. I couldn't leave him anywhere else because our separation anxiety would raise an alarm in our heads the size of Hiroshima's Geiger counter. I had no idea what to do.

I realized I stood frozen there in the middle of the room, so I turned around to look at my only hope for redemption.

The receptionist still sorted, stamped, and stapled memos on her desk, not bothering to give me the merest glance, smile, or burp by way of acknowledgement.

"So, Gertrude. How would you feel about keeping an eye on my bag while I talk to the big guy? I hate to bring it inside and clutter up the place."

She stopped working for a moment and peered at me over her glasses. "Why don't you want to bring it in with you?"

I paused and then stammered out. "I just, you know, carrying a bunch of luggage into a business meeting ... It just seems a little—"

"It's a backpack, not a hope chest." She looked back down at her desk and went on filing. "Leave it out in the waiting room. I will see that no one disturbs your—" she paused her shuffling and glanced at me again as if to punctuate the point, "backpack."

I tilted my head and thought about fessing up to my feathered friend but decided against it. Instead, I hurried over to one of the chairs in the waiting room and set it down. While I stood blocking the receptionist's view, I peeked inside and saw that Quack was indeed sound asleep.

I flopped the top closed and waved at the receptionist again. "Thanks, Bernadette. I'll be back in flash."

The door to Judas's office swung wide as soon as I got close, so I forced myself to stand up straight and march inside, hoping upon hope that when it closed Quack wouldn't feel a break in our connection or wake up ... or both.

"What took you so long? Do you have any idea what's happening in the U.S. right now?"

"I'm sorry. I had some trouble breaking away." I thought about my side trip to the infirmary and was again thankful for their speedy patch job in lieu of totaling my body and starting over. "Yes, sir, I do. Actually, I'm glad you paged me. I wanted to talk to you about something I witnessed while I was Topside."

"It had better be a way to stop this madness from spiraling any further." Judas jammed his fist into the top of his desk as he shouted out the words. Procel and Mastema were in their usual positions behind him, but neither of them so much as jumped. I was pretty sure Mastema widened her smile a little bit though.

"I sent you out there with orders to stop anything like this from happening, not to stand by and watch it happen. What have you been doing all this time?"

I moved around so I stood behind the bone chair, putting it between us as an extra measure of protection.

"With all due respect, it has only been a few hours. I did gather some valuable intel Topside, but with next to nothing to go on, I'm not sure what you expected me to do. I want to stop this as much as you do, believe me. That's my home ... Well, was my home. I don't want to see anyone destroy it. I'll figure out how to stop this thing. I promise you that."

For a second, I thought he might come over his desk at me, but instead his shoulders fell, and he lost much of his bluster. "You may be correct, Gabriel. I apologize for my haste. This has escalated so quickly it has me a bit off guard."

I nodded, a little surprised by his sudden composure. "Believe me, I get it. I was there, and I still can't believe what's happening."

"I assume you know there has been a coordinated attack on several U.S. military bases."

"Yes, like I said, I was there for one of them. Alex turned up the rest when I got back."

"What you might not be aware of is the fact that the military has mobilized against this uprising. For whatever reason, these rebels wanted to make a statement against the government. If they wanted guns, they could have stolen them from any gun shop. They hit military facilities with little to no security because they wanted to make a statement, and the U.S. military is answering in kind."

Judas steepled his fingers and tapped his chin through his beard as he spoke.

"News of the mobilization has not gone public as of yet, but with the media's propensity to sensationalize events like this, I am sure they will only drive a deeper wedge into the populous. People are choosing sides and drawing lines. It is only a matter of time before someone crosses one of them."

"I just can't believe this is all happening."

"I have seen events like this unfold before, but never have they escalated at such a rate without reason. In the past, a leader emerged to gather their legions. This appears to be unbridled madness on a scale never seen before."

"I don't know about a leader, but I did see something interesting on one of my trips up. It was a horse and rider. They were armored and had some sort of invisibility or camouflage ability. They were huge and right in the middle of the action."

I walked back around to the front of my chair feeling a little less like Judas might strangle me now. I almost felt like, dare I say, a colleague. It wouldn't last, but I was determined to enjoy it for the moment.

"I didn't see him have a direct effect on the people, but I couldn't really see him at all. No one could. I can't believe a bunch of businesspeople would pick up their staplers and hole punches and head out to attack a military facility without some sort of hoodoo bouncing around in their heads. That guy had to be controlling them somehow. If I were to bet, I would say he mobilized the gangs as his management force and the general population are his pawns. We also went up in an attempt to find this Marcella woman. We had a plan to flush her out, but it didn't go well. We managed to make a few new enemies but still don't know who she is."

I paused when I noticed Judas had dropped his hands. Usually this was when he turned red and asked me to expand on phrases like, "didn't go well" and "made a few new enemies," but he just sat in his chair, staring at me with a wide-eyed expression of what I could only describe as ... fear.

"What is it? What's wrong?" I wasn't sure what I said, but it had gone over like a sumo convention at an all you can eat buffet. Seeing Judas that taken aback had me so on edge I wanted to pick up my chair and use it as a shield. Even Mastema had lost her murderous smile and shifted uneasily on her pedestal.

"It can't be. It isn't time." He looked off into the distance without seeming to focus on anything.

"What? Time for what?" I realized I was shouting and took a breath to calm myself down. "Could you please tell me what's going on before I have an aneurism?"

Judas refocused on me and gathered his composure so fast it made me wonder if he had ever lost it in the first place.

"Forgive me. The curse of living so long is that I have a mind that sometimes wanders off on its own."

"So, what about the guy on the horse?"

"I have no idea. I think you're correct, however. A creature like that would not be there by chance. Follow up on anything you can find about this Marcella, and I will look into this horseman of yours. If I discover anything, I will page you. In the meantime, do anything you can to prevent the situation Topside from escalating."

Judas walked around his desk and for the first time ever he took me by my arm and escorted me to the door.

"Wait! You said it isn't time. What did you mean?" I tried to stop, but he used his tight grip to steer me out like a father guiding an unruly child out of a toy store. Pain kept me from putting up much of a fight. The sudden movement reminded me of my injuries the way a volcano reminded you fire was hot.

"Thank you so much for coming by. If you have anything else to report, you know how to contact me."

The door to his office opened, and he all but shoved me outside. The agitation induced another waterfall of pain in my neck and back, and I tried not to shudder as I turned around. "But..." The door had already closed, and Judas was gone.

So much for feeling like colleagues. That was more like getting bounced out of a bar for being too rowdy. He knew something, but why wasn't he telling me? I just had to hope he would get around to it later. For now, I still had Alex and Quack, and that would have to be enough. Because rider or no, I was not going to let anyone tear my home down.

CHAPTER THIRTY-SEVEN

I staggered across The Judas Agency courtyard, intending to head back to Alex's office. Turned out I didn't need to. She was on her way out of the building. When I hadn't been in the infirmary, she probably figured I had headed off to Hula Harry's or somewhere just as irresponsible. I didn't have much choice. I had to head her off.

"Alex." I shouted and double-timed it in her direction. I regretted the action immediately and slowed back down to a pace where I could maintain the bearing of a normal person.

Alex stopped, looked around, then spotted me ambling along in her direction.

"I'm glad I caught you. Where are you headed?"

"To find you." Alex glanced over my shoulder toward the building where Judas Iscariot resided. "Why were you coming from that direction?"

"I thought I saw someone I knew over there. Turns out it was just a doppelganger."

"A what?"

"A doppelganger. Someone who looks like you. Super-heroes have doppelgangers all the time. They do evil instead of good. Actually, I'm not sure which doppelganger you would be, I mean you work for The Judas Agency, so that is definitely evil, but you're trying to do some good too." I tapped my chin in contemplation.

"Next time I ask you a question like that, remind me to shove a fork in my eye instead, okay?"

"Just offering you a little trivia, that's all."

"I don't want trivia. I want to stop what's happening Topside. Did you get patched up in the infirmary?"

Alex tried to peek around me, but I leaned a shoulder against the huge depiction of Judas betraying Jesus with his infamous kiss. The statue was the centerpiece of The Judas Agency courtyard. The incredibly lifelike portrayal always gave me pause. Not because of what the statue represented but because of what it meant to me. The scene was not a betrayal, but the ultimate gift. The hardest thing anyone could have done. Judas had been the only one strong enough to make the hard choice. To do the single most important thing Jesus asked any of his disciples to do ... and he had been doing it ever since. Making hard choices to keep the real baddies from winning the show. Sometimes it was hard to remember that when he was angry enough to pull my ears off. The least I could do was help him when and where I could.

"They got me back to a semi-working condition. They said the wounds would get better over time. But it will never heal all the way, and there will always be some pain."

"They didn't try to recycle me, so I guess I'll survive. What did you find out? Was there anything to those choppers I saw flying around in L.A.?"

I already knew the answer, thanks to my visit with Judas, but I hoped Alex had found the same thing. I had no idea how to explain how I could have come by the information if all I had done was visit the infirmary.

"You were right." Alex nodded. "The National Guard is

mobilizing troops. If the civilian population continues to attack, they might kick off an all-out war. They have centralized in L.A., and they aren't the only ones. Local law enforcement noted a huge increase in gang activity there. They are smuggling reinforcements into the city, and regular people are flooding in from all over the country as well. Those who can't slip in are surrounding the city, and it's not just the fighting they're up in arms about."

Alex reached back and pulled a folded sheet of paper out of her pocket. She handed it to me, and I unfolded it to read the headline printed across the top. It said: MiRACL's Airborne Inoculation Saves Europe.

"Looks like Simeon's Smallpox cure was a success."

"What? Already?" I tried to wrap my head around the whirlwind of far-reaching events that kept happening Topside.

"I know!" Alex nodded her head. "Whether he caused the outbreak or not, his nanites saved millions of people. The bad side is, thanks to his airborne inoculation program, millions of Europeans now carry his nanites. The citizens in the U.S. see this as a direct threat. They believe the unwanted invasion is a violation of their bodies. Protesters are planning something similar to the Million-Man March, held back in 1995, but something tells me this is not going to be all that peaceful. They are going to protest MiRACL's technology and demand it be shut down, no matter the cost."

"So, what are we going to do? It's not like we command an army of undead to stop them." The thought was so cool I paused to think about that for a moment.

"You're having one of those fork-in-the-eye moments, aren't you?"

"Yes, an undead army of doppelgangers is the perfect solution."

Alex backhanded me in the chest hard enough to make me

flinch. "This is serious. There is another angle we haven't thought about, too."

"I'm almost afraid to ask."

"What if this operation is something over our heads?" she asked. "What if this entire campaign is being orchestrated by The Council of Seven?"

This was something I had already considered, but I hadn't mentioned it to her. She paused to let the thought sink in, then went on.

"Think about it. A complicated, coordinated strategy for creating death and destruction? That's The Judas Agency's back yard. We should not only know about this; we should be the ones heading it up ... unless someone higher than us is at the wheel."

I shrugged. "It's possible. The Council only answers to the big boss himself. If they're behind this, we might be considered too insignificant to inform."

I rubbed my face with my hand and then fixed Alex with a serious stare.

"That's not the real question, though. The real question is, do you care? Are we willing to try and stop this, even if this is a Council operation? Even if we know we could bring the wrath of The Council right down on our heads?"

Alex didn't hesitate. "I couldn't care less. As far as I'm concerned, we have to find a way to stop this from escalating. We can bring mountains down on our heads, and I would still do everything I can to prevent it."

I nodded. "So, we're back to the how. We still don't have an army of our own. How are we going to stop this from happening?"

"Maybe we just have to talk to the right person."

"I'm not sure talking is going to do the trick at this point. We tried that path, and I'm wearing enough ointment and non-stick gauze to moisturize a mummy."

Alex nodded. "We're going to need more aggressive negotiations for sure. We have to find Marcella and pull her out of the action in a very public way. If the gangs believe they need to negotiate for her return, they might stop fighting, at least long enough for us to come up with a better plan."

"Too bad we don't know where she is." I grumbled in frustration.

"Don't we?"

I looked up, and Alex let the statement hang in the air for a moment while she met my eyes with a wry smile.

"Come on," I said after a few seconds. "Playing the annoying partner is my gig. If you know something, fess up. Skip to the good part."

Alex let out a laugh. "You're injured, so I'll humor you. Do you remember when we stood on the mezzanine surrounded by all those bikers? When we told them we wanted to talk through a solution to all of this fighting, they laughed."

"Yeah, but I don't understand how that helps us find Marcella."

Alex sighed. "It doesn't, but one of the bikers said they should take us to Pershing Square tomorrow. They meant it as a threat, but I think Marcella might be there. It makes sense. With everything that's happening with the National Guard and the gang uprising in L.A., maybe it is all supposed to kick off tomorrow in Pershing Square."

"And Marcella is going to be there to lead the charge. Alex, you are a genius."

She shrugged and shot me a wink. "I have my moments."

I couldn't help but think how nice it was to be on the same side in this operation. Alex and I were never enemies, but she had always been on the side of destruction. Winning her over to doing something good always took a fair bit of work, and even then, I almost always had to operate under the table. It was nice to be on the same page. I just hoped it wasn't the last.

"All we have to do now is wait." I scowled at the prospect of doing nothing while our adversaries prepped for all-out war.

Alex nodded. "Like it or not, you need the rest. And if the past few hours are any indication, so does your little friend." She pointed down toward the backpack slung low on its straps. Quack was still sound asleep, and it didn't look like he had any plans to wake soon.

"Yeah." I glanced back as well. "I guess we can't make Marcella appear any faster. Let's get some sleep and head Topside early. I don't know what we're going to find, but I bet it'll be a party."

Alex nodded, and we both headed off toward our apartments. "We've faced crazier odds. At least this time there won't be any demons."

CHAPTER THIRTY-EIGHT

Alex and I had landed in Los Angeles several times over the past few days. We had seen protesters, evidence of looting and riots, and even some pretty severe vandalism. At the time, we couldn't believe people would cause so much destruction in their own city. This morning we had landed to make our way to Pershing Square, and the streets of Los Angeles didn't look like a city at all.

"What have they done to this place?" I peered out an alley and onto the street. It was so early the sun had barely made an appearance, but there was still plenty to see. The area seemed abandoned of any visible life, but overturned cars, trailers, and concrete barricades created a bottleneck to anyone foolish enough to venture out. The mirrored glass windows and department store displays had all been shattered on the first and second floors, giving the buildings a ragged, toothy look. I remembered seeing an old movie depicting an Italian city after the Germans had rolled through it in WWII. There were bricks, broken buildings, and rubble everywhere. The city's desperation, anger, and hate were almost palpable. This was the same thing. L.A. was a war zone, silent and waiting. The only thing left to do was bleed.

Alex went to step off into the street, but I reached out to put a hand on the shoulder of her long overcoat. We had both changed into our Topside gear as a waterproof deterrent to any Super Soaker wielding gang members. She had her dark coat and thigh-high boots, and I wore my Gore-Tex pants and jacket. A patchwork brown and orange ensemble gaudy enough to make any hiker green with envy. I had zipped on the matching hood to afford me a bit more head protection, but it felt too little too late. The ruined skin on my scalp, neck, and back hissed with pain every time I moved. I only wished I had taken the precaution earlier. I didn't know how long I would be like this, but even if I did heal, I didn't think I would ever be the same.

"I don't think wandering into the open is going to be our smartest move here. I bet they have snipers set up all over the place. We want to find Marcella, not get shot."

Alex nodded. "Any suggestions on how to do that?"

My backpack rustled, and Quack popped his head out of the top and stretched his black beak in a little ducky yawn.

"*Wow, what happened to this place? I take a little nap, and the whole world falls apart.*"

"A little nap?" I said. "You slept through half the day yesterday. I started to think you were dead."

Quack scoffed. "*I was a little stressed. Excuse me. Now, where are we, and why is everything broken? Actually, never mind that. What are we doing here, and please don't tell me you are doing something stupid?*"

I turned my head away and scanned the street ahead of us.

"We're just here to chat with the one responsible for putting this party together."

"*Do me a favor.*" Quack sounded so matter of fact we both paused to pay attention. "*Stop and listen to your surroundings for a second. Do you hear any birds chirping, dogs barking, or cats meowing? Are there even any bugs buzzing around your face right now?"*

Alex and I took in the eerie silence.

"No," I said. "Nothing. What's your point?"

"My point is people are stupid. There's a reason animals head for the hills when a tsunami makes its way to shore. They know when it's time to get out of the way. Not even a fruit fly is dumb enough to be standing where you are right now, yet here you are."

Alex let out a laugh. "You are one smart duck."

"Forgive me for intruding, but I believe your feathered friend is right."

Alex and I both spun toward the voice emerging from the shadows behind us. Sammy materialized in the alley somehow and walked our way. She didn't have her usual cynical smirk. This time she moved with a purpose and wore a look of concern.

"I fear this is going to be a battle no one can win. Being here will only get you ... Well, killed isn't quite the word I'm looking for, but I'm sure you don't like the idea of what happens if you're caught in the crossfire of a fight like this."

"We heal, remember?" Alex sneered. "Their guns might hurt us, but they aren't going to do any lasting damage."

"There are wounds other than physical. And don't forget someone here knows your weakness. If you're recognized again, you might find yourself facing down a weapon tailor made for wayward Niners."

"Duly noted, but that doesn't change anything," I said. "We have to find Marcella and try to stop this. Right now, I think she might be the only one who can."

Sammy rubbed her temples with the palms of her hands. "Yes, but you are forgetting one thing. This is not your problem. They caused it. Let them reap the consequences."

"That seems like a very un-angelic thing to say." Alex raised an eyebrow at her then turned her gaze back to the street.

Sammy sighed and took a step backward. "My place is but to observe and act only if I am told to do so. Otherwise, I am obligated to allow humankind to act upon their greatest gift. Free will."

Sammy turned away and walked back toward the dumpsters deep in the shadowed alleyway. "I will be here watching, but I cannot interfere. I suggest you do the same."

With that, she burst into her pigeon form and flew away.

"Uh, I hope you don't mind, but I think I'm going to follow her lead," Quack said. *"I have an allergy to buckshot. I'll fly high over you two and keep an eye on things from up there."*

I took the backpack off and let Quack out to stretch his wings. "That's a good idea. We'll see you when this is all over."

Quack ran several steps on his webbed feet then took off.

And then it was two.

"Well," I said. "Shall we head down this bottleneck and find our little oasis in the sand?"

Alex rolled her eyes and stepped around the corner, this time staying closer to the building. "Come on. Let's get this over with."

I followed in behind her and wondered about the wisdom of our plan. Sammy had a point. Marcella seemed to know our every weakness, but we didn't even know what she looked like. If anyone recognized us, we would be rainwater goo before we had a chance to say two words.

Pershing Square was a park set among miles of smog, asphalt, and glass. A slice of natural heaven in a great, big chunk of man-made hell. It seemed ironic that Marcella would launch her offensive from such a place. Not only did it offer a tactical disadvantage by being open and less defensible, it was also a place of peace in a city made of chaos. I just hoped she would be in a position for us to surprise her. Alex and I were done announcing our arrival. We would get in and get out before her troops had a chance to pivot to a defense that could harm us. If we couldn't do that ... well, there was always Plan B.

As we walked through the city, I felt eyes on me from everywhere. I couldn't see anyone hiding among the makeshift bunkers and barricades, but there was no doubt they were there. The silence felt like an entity all its own, so when a sound broke through in the distance to foretell the inevitable, it was all the more alarming. I'd heard the noise only in movies, but the sound was unmistakable.

The high, keening cry of tank treads echoed off the buildings. They sounded like they came from everywhere. The military troops advanced. The battleground was set. I couldn't believe what I was about to witness. A bloody clash among brothers, fathers, sons, mothers, daughters, and sisters. No one would be left out. Our country would go to war with itself, and there was nothing I could do to stop it.

I looked over at Alex, and her expression of despair matched my own. We had come too late. This would happen, and all we could do was watch.

I stared out at the street and scanned the buildings around us, hoping for some sort of inspiration. We were so close. Pershing Square was only a few blocks away. None came, but something else did. It was the familiar feeling I recognized from the battle at the Armory. That perception that I had missed something. An impression that someone was near, but I couldn't see them.

I squinted my eyes and stared out at the expanse of wreckage strewn blacktop, trying to notice any places I did not ... could not look. I sensed it almost immediately, just fifty yards away at the end of the bottlenecked street.

I tried to concentrate all my attention in the area, but there were too many visual distractions in between. I couldn't focus. Then I noticed something else. Something heavy in my pocket.

I reached inside and felt the small flashlight I had found earlier.

I pulled it out and stared at the chromed surface a moment, then realization dawned on me. The flashlight was not a trinket from Quack's collection, it was an item formed from the power of the Denarius. My coin offered specialized abilities when I needed them. They were never the most practical items, but they did seem to be the exact items I needed to do the job at hand.

I clicked the flashlight on and shined it in the direction of the anomaly. The second the unseen beam hit it, the Horse and rider came into view.

They stood there, restless in their oversized armor. He did indeed wear a bone helmet and mask. The faceplate, I hadn't noticed before, was human. The horse's eyes glowed red, and as it turned to look at us, he seemed to sense the fact that we had exposed him. His mount reared back, and the rider raised his arm, revealing a broadsword in his hand. The blade was raven black and looked as if it had been snapped off about a third of the way down, leaving a jagged end rather than a sharp point.

As I held the light on him, he turned his horse, and with a violent kick of his heels, he charged straight at us.

CHAPTER THIRTY-NINE

Watching the horse and rider charge us under the view of the flashlight was like watching a charging grizzly through a pinhole in a tent flap. If I moved at all, the beam lost its target, and the horse and rider disappeared. I had only a moment to react, so I jabbed Alex in the shoulder to wake her out of her shock, then shoved the flashlight into her hand.

"Hold this steady. We can't see him without it."

The sound of beating hooves and panting breath began to fill my ears as the horse got closer and the rider leaned down, leveling his broken sword toward my head.

Time for Plan B. I tore off my jacket and revealed my ace in the hole.

"You brought a Hellion weapon Topside?" Alex shrieked. "Have you lost your mind?"

I yanked my Whip Crack out of its over the shoulder holster and had just enough time to let it play out next to me. The Whip Crack was an unholy cross between a bullwhip and a chainsaw. It was my favorite weapon, and used correctly, all but impossible to defend against. I flicked my wrist to engage the blades and snapped it out toward my attacker's waiting sword arm. He tried to pull back at the last second, but it was too late. I caught him around his forearm gauntlet and yanked the blades tight. They slashed at his armor with a whine of gears and grating steel. Sparks flew, and I dug my heels in as they passed, bracing for the backlash.

The rider tried to stop his mount, but he couldn't react fast enough. I had out maneuvered him for a second time. The Whip Crack snapped tight and yanked the rider off his saddle, bringing him to the asphalt in a crash of steel and bone.

For one moment, everything fell to a strained hush. It was as if the world waited to see what would happen next. Then everything exploded into a hail of bullets and explosions, and the battle for Los Angeles was on.

I struggled to free my Whip Crack from the rider's arm, but the rider rolled over and clamped his armored glove over the top of it, locking it into place. The weapon had sliced through the heavy plating, but not enough to make a clean cut. On anything else, that arm would be lying on the ground, and I would be rearing back for another attack. But he had my only weapon seized up, and I couldn't pull it free. If I couldn't retrieve my Whip Crack, Alex and I would be sitting ducks. I had to assume the rider's sword was as deadly as anything Alex or I could have brought up from The Nine. This guy was no typical Topsider, so I had little doubt his hardware was at least as good as mine.

I had also noticed something else. As he got to his feet, the rider was no longer camouflaged or cloaked within his power. He had lost his ratty, green cape. It laid in a heap behind him, and now that I saw it clearly, the thing looked more like a tarp or a cheap piece of plastic. Not at all fitting for the high-tech armor ensemble he wore. Then again, if the cape kept him hidden, who cared what it looked like?

The rider stood toe to toe with me among ear shattering gunfire and shrieking mortar rounds. Neither of us tried to duck the melee. The rider looked much shorter than I had expected now that he was on the ground. Despite all his armor, he had a small stature as well. I studied the overall shape and movement of my enemy, and realized I faced not a man, but a woman. That was something I hadn't expected. An armor-clad female warrior who now stood upright and ready to take my head off.

The rider yanked at the Whip Crack, and the handle came sailing out of my hand. In my surprise, I had loosened my grip enough to allow her to pull it away.

This was not a good way to start.

"Alex, I could use a little help!" I shouted over the noise, not wanting to take my eyes off my opponent.

No response. I risked a quick glance to the side, only to see Alex and my fancy rider revealing flashlight were gone. My heart sank. I was on my own. I decided I could not worry about her right now. I had bigger problems to deal with.

Small arms fire, RPGs, and mortars boomed up and down the street. People died by the dozens, and sulfurous smoke and muzzle flashes made it almost impossible to see. The sounds of war echoed in the canyon of the city streets, yet the only thing that mattered was this rider. Somehow, I knew. She was the one. She was responsible for all of this. Kill her, and the fever pitch of this battle would die. The bloodlust would disappear, and they could all go about picking up the pieces.

I circled her, looking for any opening, any weakness she might have. I had no weapon, no armor, no nothing, but I had to find a way. If she would just drop my Whip Crack.

As if in answer, she reached over and took the time to coil up my weapon. She handled it with the ease of someone who had used something similar before, then dropped it at her feet. I couldn't see her face behind that hideous bone mask, but if I could, I had a feeling she would be smiling.

She raised her broken sword in front of her, then took a step in my direction. I wasn't sure if she expected me to run, but I had no intention of retreating. Instead, I reached down and hefted a large piece of concrete and threw it at her head. She dodged it at the last second, but not before it glanced off her shoulder, leaving a concrete dust smudge on her armor.

She looked over at the smudge, then back at me.

"Not smiling now are you, Bit—"

Before I could finish, she charged, sword in high guard and ready to rain down a killing blow.

I backpedaled, my eyes searching everywhere for a weapon, anything that would save me—a stick, a gun, a feral cat. My back was to an overturned car, and there was no room to run. She had me dead to rights, so I did the only thing I could do. I flipped her the bird and got ready to die. I found I could barely keep my eyes open. I didn't want to see the end coming, but I forced myself to do it anyway. I was glad I had. If I hadn't, I would have missed seeing the orange Dodge Charger broadside the rider just before she got a chance to swing her sword down and cleave my head in two.

There was a horrific screech of metal, then a crash as the car careened into the side of a brick wall, pancaking the rider between it and the big, square grill on the front of the car. That was enough to make me turn my head away. I didn't want to see the aftermath of that mess. A second later the car door opened, and Alex jumped out to run toward me.

"Gabe!" She grabbed me in a tight hug, then stepped back to look at me. I cringed at her arms pulling tight across my neck but tried not to show it.

"I can't believe you're still alive. I thought he had you. I'm sorry it took me so long. The rioters destroyed every car for blocks. I was lucky to find one I could use as a battering ram."

I nodded. "Well, if you wanted to cut it close, you couldn't have done it any better. Thanks, partner." I exhaled, trying to pull myself back together.

"What was that thing? And please tell me he was the only one," Alex shouted over the noise of the ongoing battle.

The horrific thought that the rider might not be alone had never occurred to me. I hoped there wasn't any more of those things. If there were, we would need a lot more cars.

I moved closer to her, so I wouldn't have to yell. "I think that was the only one. And it wasn't a he, I'm pretty sure it was a she."

More gunfire zinged overhead, and we both ducked.

"Maybe we should find some cover."

I nodded again. "I know this sounds crazy, but I thought all of this would end if we killed her."

I rushed over to grab my Whip Crack then ran back to Alex again.

"I figured she had some sort of power over these people. I thought taking her out of the equation would bring these people back to their senses."

Alex pointed to the front of the car where she had pinned the rider to the outside of the building.

"Maybe it would have." She grabbed my shoulders and turned me around.

The rider was gone. She had not only survived the crash somehow but had pushed the car out of the way and made her escape as well. Her cape and horse were missing too.

"Damn it." I searched all around us and took Alex by the arm, pulling her off the street and into an alcove where we could be safe for a moment.

"At least we don't have to worry about finding Marcella anymore."

I frowned at her trying to understand.

"Don't you get it. The rider's a woman. Marcella seems to be responsible for this confrontation. If the rider is leading any part of this, it only makes sense that the rider is Marcella."

I smacked my head with my palm.

"So stupid. I can't believe I didn't put that together."

"You were a little busy."

I chuckled. "Do you still have my flashlight?"

"No. I put it down, and then I couldn't find it aga—"

I reached into my pocket and retrieved the very same flashlight. Most of the time, I didn't appreciate the "can never be lost" nuance of the Denarius, but right now, I wouldn't trade it for anything in the world.

"How did you do that?" Alex peered at me as if I had just pulled off the perfect magic trick at her cousin's Bar Mitzvah.

"Never mind, I'll explain later." I wouldn't, or if she remembered, I would have to come up with a fabulous lie. The last thing I could do was explain the truth about the coin and the Denarii Division.

"Just keep this light peeled in the area all around us. She can't hide as long as we use that. If we're going to end this thing, our only option is to destroy her."

CHAPTER FORTY

O ur plan needed several things to work, most of which would be all but impossible to make happen. The main ingredient was Marcella. Without her, we didn't have a party. We searched high and low, then found her at the heart of the most vicious fighting in the city.

We watched her from the cover of a nearby building. Marcella stood in the middle of a wide street, flanked on either side by high-rise buildings. Everything was in ruins, and I had a very real concern that all the structural damage could bring one of the huge buildings down around us. Glass, concrete, brick, and steel lay everywhere in rubbled heaps. Bullets sailed through the air like swarms of mosquitoes, threatening to consume anyone foolish enough to wander into their path. It was a war zone like none I had ever seen, and we were smack dab in the middle of it.

"Are you ready for this?" I looked over at Alex and raised an eyebrow.

"I'm not the one sitting on a fishhook offering myself up as bait."

I shrugged. "It'll be worth it, if the plan works."

"And if it doesn't?"

I shook my head. "It's going to work. Now go get ready. I have to go tempt our fish."

Alex started to walk away, then turned back to me, and before I could do anything to react, she pulled me in for a kiss. I reeled at the sentiment, wanting to put my arms around her and make the moment last, but Alex backed away.

"For luck."

I smiled. "All of a sudden, I feel like the luckiest guy in The Nine."

Alex rolled her eyes, but I saw her blush beneath all that dismissiveness. "Just don't get caught, little worm. I'll be ready when you are."

I watched her run off until she was out of sight then pushed off the wall and headed out as well.

I had the special flashlight in my hand, but I wasn't using it —not yet. Once we found Marcella, we didn't want to risk her knowing we were up to something. I depended on that sensation of not seeing. That sense that something was there even though it remained elusive to the eye. As long as I had that, I knew Marcella was close by.

A stray bullet hit me in the shoulder, spinning me around in a white-hot shot of pain. I was again thankful that we healed almost instantly up here. Alex and I had both been hit several times, but there was no real damage. I would expel that bullet and heal up before they said the word ricochet. I wished I could say as much for my other injuries. I kept up a good front for Alex, but the constant burn and ache was wearing on me. Having such an injury made it hard to move, and considering I was about to go up against a medieval tank, being less than one hundred percent seemed tantamount to suicide.

Ready or not, it was time to announce my presence in the main event and ring the bell for round two.

Gunfire slowed, and I concentrated on figuring out where

Marcella stood. It didn't take long to find her. I shined my flashlight off to my right and sure enough, there she was. Marcella hadn't noticed me yet and didn't seem to be aware that she was in the spotlight again. She drew her sword from her scabbard, and all at once, I heard both sides of the battle roar to life. They shouted out words of hate and malice at one another, then all at once, the hail of unstoppable bullets reached a fever pitch again, pounding each other with relentless savagery.

I studied Marcella from across the street, watching as she commanded her legions atop her armored mount. She did not seem to care which side won as long as both of them fought. She may have started with the gangs, then the throng of civilians, but now she commanded them all. Turning each side against the other. She was nothing more than a catalyst. A horseman bent on ...

That's when it hit me. The thing Judas would not say. I knew what Marcella was ... or at least I thought I did. To be honest, I hoped I was wrong. If I wasn't, we had zero chance of succeeding with our plan. There was only one way to find out.

I launched out of my position while Marcella's back was turned and charged before she had a chance to react. My Whip Crack landed a vicious attack on the shoulder joint of her armor. I hoped the plating would be thinner there, and the Whip Crack would be less likely to get hung up. The attack got her attention because I heard a high-pitched scream emit from beneath that bone mask. It was a shout of pure pain and rage.

She spun her horse around to face me, and I didn't hesitate. I launched several more attacks at her, all at her vulnerable joints rather than the thick, armored hide. I missed most of the time, but I did manage another hit on her right knee. Her hand went down out of instinct to protect it. She doubled over in pain now, but I wasn't stupid enough to believe I had her on the ropes. I had used a Hellion weapon on her, so she couldn't heal, but she was no pushover. She proved me right seconds later.

Marcella heeled her mount forward in a sudden charge of armored muscle. I dove to the side just in time to avoid being trampled, but she was already rounding on me again as she drew her broken sword to cut me down.

Time to run.

I turned and sprinted a few yards away from her, then ducked and dodged again, avoiding her attacks by inches. I used the flashlight to see her and my Whip Crack to keep her off balance whenever I could, but she had the clear advantage in this fight. I launched an attack at her face, then ran again.

Marcella flinched, but as soon as she recovered, she ran me down. This time she wasn't fast enough. I turned into a narrow alley between buildings, preventing her from having a straight shot at me. The downside to my maneuver was that I had trapped myself. Heavy brick walls surrounded me on both sides, and there was no exit at the far end. The narrow width of the alley prevented her from getting a good swing with her sword, but if she decided to run me down with her warhorse, there wasn't much I could do.

I sprinted to the far end as fast as my legs would carry me. At least standing next to a wall would make it tougher for her to trample my body—maybe. To be honest, I had no idea. I knew nothing about armored knights and even less about warhorses. Marcella guided her mount into the alley and darkened the entrance with their impressive bulk. As I shined my flashlight on them, she turned her mount sideways to take up the entire space from wall to wall. It was a cheap intimidation tactic. It also worked. If there had been a way to claw my way up these bricks like a rabid cat, I would have done it.

Marcella turned to face me then guided her horse about halfway down the alley before dismounting. She didn't bother grabbing the reins. As she walked ahead, the horse followed like a loyal Labrador.

Gunfire, mortar rounds, and RPG explosions rocked the

area outside the alley. The noise was deafening. Inside the echoing walls, it was almost debilitating. I stood there with my Whip Crack, waiting for her to close in. I had to time this just right. Too soon and she would escape. Too early and ...

She took one more step, and I launched myself forward. Not at her, but toward a small door built into the brick wall. Marcella began to realize her mistake and charged as I jerked it open, but she was too late. I kicked the rock that had held the door ajar and yanked it closed again.

I had only seconds depending on what she did next. I ran as fast as I could through the abandoned backroom of a clothing store. There were racks and mannequins stacked along the wall, but Alex and I had cleared a path for me to get through. When I popped out another door toward the front of the alley, I saw that Alex had done her job as well. She had shoved two big, green dumpsters into the narrow access, essentially blocking Marcella's retreat. The noise of the battle had more than covered the rumble of the dumpsters, and a couple of makeshift wheel chocks would make it all but impossible to move them back again. They now stood lengthwise, taking up the full width of the alley as a double deep barricade against Marcella's retreat. She would have to climb over them both in order to escape, and there was no way she could do that on her horse.

Alex stood on the rear most dumpster facing a no doubt furious Marcella.

"She's climbing up." Alex's voice sounded more than a little panicked.

"Do it. I'm right behind you."

Alex put her hands out and closed her eyes in concentration. A flame erupted from her palms, shooting out like a torch. I was only a few yards away, but I ran for all I was worth.

Marcella had clambered halfway onto the first dumpster

and drew her sword arm back to strike just as I caught Alex's left ankle with my hand.

I poured my power into her, and all at once, her meager torch transformed into a torrent of white-hot fire. The wall of flame hit Marcella like a truck, forcing her back down to the ground. She let out a terrible scream, and I feared Alex might relent, but I was glad she didn't. Instead, she poured even more power into her assault. I shielded my face with my other arm and dared a peek into the alley. Everything was on fire. I had never seen anything like it. Flames rolled along the ground and up the side of the building like a living being while Alex bombarded the center with her power.

She held it like that for what felt like an eternity. The dumpster before us turned orange, then white. The air was so hot it became almost impossible to breathe. Then all at once, Alex cut her power off. She took in gasp and let her shoulders slump as she squinted down into the glowing slag in the alley.

"If she can live through that, she deserves to take over the world." Alex turned to me and crouched down, reaching out so I could help her off the dumpster.

I grabbed her hand and guided her down. "I know I've said this before, but seriously, remind me never to piss you off."

Alex chuckled. "That wasn't all me, and you know it. How did you know we could combine our powers like that?"

"I didn't really. I just remembered that day you melted those guns into slag." Alex had saved us from a band of railroad bandits a few months ago by turning all their guns to goo. Until now, we never understood how.

"I had my hand on your shoulder that day. There have been other times too. Like the day in the shipyard when your fireball went haywire. It all made me think about how our powers might work together. I can rust metal or oxidize it. I'm eroding the steel by infusing it with oxygen somehow. I figured the reason for your turbo charged flame was me. My oxidizing power boosts your fire power like a shot of nitrous in a street racer. We work synergistically."

"Whoa. Slow down, Dr. Chemistry. You'll hurt your brain with big words like that."

"Synergistically is going to be my new buzzword. Our partnership works synergistically." I grinned.

"Your stupidity works synergistically with your mouth."

"Now you're getting it," I said. "Maybe just leave out the insult part."

"But it's nowhere near as funny." Alex pointed up toward the street. "Sounds like your theory about Marcella may have been right too. The fighting has pretty much stopped."

We had been so involved with Marcella I hadn't even noticed that the gunfire had all but ceased. No more explosions or mortar fire. Now that all the fighting was done, another sound filled the air. It was not as loud as the battle but every bit as disturbing. Everywhere people cried out for help. Wounded on both sides moaned and shouted. It grew until the constant drone of wailing injured was almost worse than the fight.

"We should go help where we can." I started toward the street and Alex nodded in agreement. "I'm right behind you."

Alex started toward me, but before I turned around, I saw movement over the top of the dumpster. I lunged forward and yanked Alex out of the way just as Marcella let out a furious scream and crested the top, a steaming heap of armor and burned flesh. Her broken sword came down in a streak of smoking black steel, and before I could move out of the way, it plunged through my chest, driving me to my knees.

CHAPTER FORTY-ONE

I opened my eyes to see Alex looking down on me. I was lying on my back, still breathing the heated remnants of the fire Alex and I had used to try and destroy Marcella.

"Don't try to move." She had her hand on my cheek. It was slick and wet. "You're going to be okay." Tears streamed out of her eyes, and I knew she was lying.

"Listen to me." I choked out the words and every syllable felt like hot lead in my lungs. "Don't go after her. She's too powerful. I wasn't sure ..."

"What?" Alex began to rock back and forth. I didn't have the heart to tell her the movement felt like grating sandpaper into my wound. I was just happy she was still alive.

"Where is she? Where ..." I coughed.

"She ran. We hurt her pretty bad, but she's not dead. Not yet." The murderous tone in her voice broke through the panic and sorrow for a moment, but then she looked back down at me, not bothering to wipe away the tears now streaming down her face. "I can't believe we didn't kill her. Gabe, I'm so sorry."

"It's not your fault." I tried to stifle another cough. "We

didn't know. Remind me. When I get out of the Pools. After I suffer through the Gnashing Fields. Remind me."

"Remind you of what? I don't understand." Her voice was frantic, and I began to see darkness creep around the side of my vision. "Gabe! Stay with me!"

"Marcella. She's a Horseman."

"Okay. I'll remind you about Marcella and her horse, I promise. Whatever you want, just don't die. I need you." She sobbed, almost uncontrollably.

I shook my head and coughed. "No. She's a Horseman. One of the Four Horseman. She is War. Don't fight her. Remind me."

Alex said something else, but I couldn't hear. She was too far away. Darkness took me, and my soul sunk deep into the screaming torture of the Gnashing Fields.

THANKS FOR READING!

Did you love War Origin? Join the C.G. Harris Legion to stay up to date on upcoming books, receive book intel, useless trivia, special giveaways, plus you'll learn about Hula Harry and get his Drink of the Week. https://www.cgharris.net/legion-sign-up-page

Let other readers know what you thought of, War Origin, by Leaving a Review

Book 5, the final book in The Judas Files series, is expected to release in the fall of 2021

———————

Haven't read the other books in The Judas File series? Get them now:

Book 1-THE NINE

Book 2-NEW DOMINION

Book 3-ARTFUL EVIL

ABOUT THE AUTHOR

C.G. Harris is an award winning science-fiction and fantasy author from Colorado who draws inspiration from favorites, Jim Butcher, Richard Kadrey and Brandon Sanderson. For nearly a decade, Harris has escaped the humdrum of the real world by creating fictional characters and made-up realities. When not writing, Harris spends time collecting the illusive arcade token, from the golden age when Dig Dug and Frogger were king. Harris knows the value of such a collection will only be seen in the confused faces of those family members left behind long after C.G. Harris is gone.

Do you have questions, comments or ideas for future plot lines in the Judas Files series? Contact C.G. at: CGharrisAuthor@gmail.com